JUDGE
MENT
DAVE

PRAISE FOR JUDGEMENT DAVE

Clarke has keen insight, and *Judgment Dave* holds up a mirror to our present moment ... a hilarious tale wrapped around a warm, uplifting core.

- J. SCOTT COATSWORTH, AUTHOR OF *THE STARK DIVIDE*

Read this if you love queer space romps that have something important to say – and can still make you laugh.

- ALEX, ACROSS MY SHELVES

Joining the *Teapot* crew again is like snuggling in a fuzzy blanket. It's just so wholesome and lovely.

- MAUREEN, GOODREADS USER

A pleasure to read ... filled with thrills and spills and good old-fashioned fun.

- JOHN DEREK, GOODREADS USER

For everyone who's still wearing a mask, who's still social-distancing, and who still believes in science.

JUDGEMENT DAVE

A TALE OF APAWCALYPTIC PROPORTIONS

SI CLARKE

Judgement Dave

Print edition ISBN 978-1-7397681-0-2

ebook edition ISBN 978-1-9162878-9-1

www.whitehartfiction.co.uk

Most recent update: 1 January 2022

Editing by:

- Michelle Meade of Michelle Meade Reads
- Lucy York of Lucy Rose York
- Hannah McCall of Black Cat Editorial Services

Cover illustration by: Vadim Sadovski

Black and white illustration by: Ricardo Mossini

❀ Created with Vellum

AUTHOR'S NOTE

This book is written in British English. If you're used to reading American English, some of the spelling and punctuation may seem unusual. I promise, it's totally safe.

This story also features a number of Canadianisms. Sadly, I cannot promise these are safe. You may find yourself involuntarily wearing a touque and craving Timbits and a double-double. It can't be helped. Seek treatment immediately.

Lastly, this book contains an inordinate number of geek culture references. This as an homage to all things science fiction. There are countless references to all my favourites – *Star Trek*, *Red Dwarf*, *Firefly*, *The X-Files*, *Doctor Who*, *Battlestar Galactica*, *Hitchhiker's Guide to the Galaxy*, *Babylon 5*, *The Expanse*, etc. None of it should be read as derogatory or dismissive, nor would I ever suggest my work can take the place of anyone else's. Please support artists and authors. This is my love song to the entire genre.

CONTENT WARNINGS

This work contains the following:

- Slavery, oppression, and genocide
- Ableism

Also, please note that trans women are women. Trans men are men. Non-binary people are who they tell you they are. This book is not for TERFs.

PREVIOUSLY ON STARSHIP TEAPOT...

Okay, you know how in TV shows you get that little one-minute segment at the start of each episode to catch you up? Books should do that too, I think. Just a handy little reminder since it may have been a while since you read the first one.

———

Previously on *Starship Teapot*... [You may want to imagine Anthony Stewart Head's voice reading this to you.]

Lem, a perfectly ordinary aro-ace agender IT project manager, is kidnapped by aliens while camping with her German shepherd, Spock. While trying to figure out how to get home, they make some new friends: a talking horse-person, an unswearing robot, an overly anxious parrot, and a cloud of sentient glitter gas. Along the way, Lem discovers that the universe is far stranger than she'd ever imagined.

I struggled to think how I was going to explain this. 'My people wear clothes – like armour, but soft. It protects us and

keeps us warm. Also, we don't generally walk around naked,
even if the temperature would allow it.'

One of the things Lem learns is that Darmok and Jalad
were right: communication requires a shared frame of reference. So, Holly, Lem's universal translator and personal AI,
suggests using figurative mode to facilitate easier discourse.

'This will include facts you already know but may have
forgotten,' it explained. 'I will also incorporate extrapolative
and fictional sources. Your extensive knowledge of science
fiction will provide a useful base for figurative mode.'

Early on in her new life in space, Lem encounters an
alien.

She raised her arms. Wait, his arms? Their arms? I shook
my head. Not the time to wonder about alien pronouns. I
decided to stick with she until someone told me otherwise.

Much later, Lem learns that alien sex and gender are …
complicated. The binary most people are used to on Earth
doesn't apply.

'Hang on,' I said. 'If pronouns don't align to sex or gender
because most species don't think that way… Does that mean
BB, Aurora, and Henry aren't women?'

So there are two pronouns: *she* for all sentient beings and
it for all non-sentient/inanimate objects. And as for names…

'Back in the early days of translators, programmers tried to
transliterate names of people and places,' said Bexley. 'But it

*was all "unintelligible noise this" and "awkward silence that".
No, in the end, they decided the best thing for it was for people
to make their own names for everyone they encounter. Once
you assign a name to someone, your AI will remember it.'*

That's right: it's literally impossible to misgender or dead-
name someone. Whatever you may call a person, the translator will convert it to their preferred name or pronoun. Lem
names her new best friend, a horse-person, Bexley because…

'When I was a kid, we went to go' – do not say riding, *I
instructed myself* – *'meet them in a place called Bexley.
That's it. I'll call you Bexley. What do you think? Is that
okay?'*

After two kidnappings and three escapes, Lem and the
gang escape and meet up in the pub.

*'A horse, an unswearing robot, a giant parrot, a cloud of
sentient glitter gas, a non-binary IT project manager, and a
talking dog walk into a bar,' I began.*

And when it's finally time to go home, Lem and Spock
decide that, actually, they're more at home in this weird and
wonderful universe than they ever were on Earth.

1 / LIZARD IN THE BASEMENT

'Byeeeeeeee!'

Bexley and I smiled and waved as we clicked the button to shut the door – then we turned to face the carnage our guests had left in the cargo bay. Overturned crates lay at all angles, their contents splayed out everywhere. Dirty dishes – some of which were broken – littered every surface. Blankets and mattresses were strewn about the entire space. And the smell! It was like rotten meat, stale beer, and … something vaguely like popcorn?

I collapsed to the floor with my back against the door. Spock, my German shepherd, leaned against me and whimpered softly. I buried my hand in her soft fur.

Bexley gently stroked my hair. 'Come on, Lem. Let's head to the mess hall.' She took a step back. Looking down her long, horsey nose, she offered a hoof to help me up.

We'd all voted to accept the job – ferrying a gaggle of hormonal adolescents to their species' ancestral home planet – but I doubted we'd ever take another job from the trelane. Or was it unfair to judge an entire species by how their teenagers behaved?

'I'm trying not to look at the damage,' I said as we plodded towards the lift.

Bexley tapped her hooves in the air – her version of a nod. 'I'm too exhausted to even think about cleaning up.'

I blew out noisily through my lips – like a nickering horse. 'Same. But at least with cleaning, I can pretend I have as much to contribute as the rest of you.'

Bexley chewed the air thoughtfully. 'What? How do you mean? You contribute. We need to work on your self-confidence. I don't understand why you're always so down on yourself.'

'I *help*,' I said. 'Or at least, I try. But you... You're a genius mechanic. Henry's a pilot. BB's a doctor.'

Bexley stopped walking and blocked my path. 'And Aurora takes care of our supplies and domestic needs. Spock looks after our physical security. And you ... do whatever needs doing.'

I raised my hands in – I don't know: exasperation? Frustration? Vindication? 'See! You totally paused. I don't know what my responsibility is. You don't know. No one does. I don't have a responsibility. There's nothing I offer that couldn't be done by pretty much any warm body.'

Bexley's ears swivelled like pointy little satellite dishes as we started walking again. 'What does your core temperature have to do—' She waved her arms in front of herself. 'Whatever. You're good at stuff. And you're my best friend. We all value you – even Henry.'

I pulled a face. 'Henry doesn't believe I'm sapient.' I pressed the button to call the lift.

'Well, okay,' she admitted. 'That might be true, actually. But it's completely beside the point. And anyways, you do stuff. You definitely contribute. Like, as much as anyone. And did I mention you're my best friend? Because you totally are. I mean, I know I say that about a lot of people, but I really, really—'

The lift door slid open, revealing a smooth blue cylinder sitting on the floor, seething. Henry. Someone had graffitied her casing. At least I hoped it was paint.

'Oh, Henry,' whispered Bexley. 'I'm so sorry, honey. They did this to you?'

'No, I got bored with the basic blue and hit up a salon for a colour upgrade.' Henry's poshly accented gender-neutral voice dripped with scorn. 'Of course they did this to me, you pickling buffoon.'

Even the lift was littered with assorted rubbish. One of the walls was smeared with… 'What even is that?'

'I wouldn't if I were you, sandwich,' Henry said as my fingers were mere centimetres from the substance.

Turning to face her, I asked, 'Did you analyse the contents?'

Spock licked the wall.

'I look like a mobile cuffing crime lab to you?' An appendage that looked bizarrely like a spork flipped down from her normally featureless shape and sort of stabbed at me. 'It's no skin off my nose if you want to touch whatever bodily fluid or waste material that might be.' The spork folded back into her cylindrical form. 'Not that I even have a nose. Or skin.'

Figurative mode strikes again. Holly, my AI, translated everyone's words into English for me. Sometimes it produced strange colloquialisms – not because the people speaking happened to have the same sayings – but because Holly used the nearest corollary my mind contained.

Bexley's lips pulled back from her massive equine teeth. 'I swear, if I never see another trelane it'll be too soon.'

Spock let out a heavy love-struck sigh as the lift door opened.

'Come on,' I said, gently steering her towards the mess. Spock whined in protest. 'We'll see if we can rustle you up some treats, eh?'

At that, her ears perked up and … well, she may have plodded a bit less slowly the rest of the way.

The ship was sized for beings much shorter than your typical human. Thankfully, the ceilings were high enough for me to walk around comfortably … but the doorways were another matter, so when the door slid open, I had to duck to get through. I stumbled over nothing as I entered the room.

Aurora gasped. Beside her, BB let out a squawk as she plucked a golden feather from her chest with her beak. As she let it fall to the floor I noticed little bald patches all over her body.

Aurora's normal rainbow hues faded until she was almost invisible. Generally, she looked like an amorphous blob of rainbow glitter gas – with different colours receding or rising to prominence, indicating her moods. 'Dear me. You lot gave me a start.'

'Those catting uncles,' Henry unswore. 'No barking trelane is ever setting foot on my— on *this* ship again. Never.'

Bexley stroked a hoof over Henry's lid in a soothing sort of gesture. She reached her other arm out towards BB, but BB stepped backwards into Aurora's … well, into Aurora. BB turned her head away from us and buried it in her own shoulder feathers.

I felt helpless. Much of my life had been wasted feeling helpless. I didn't like the feeling. Everyone was upset. The last few weeks had left us all anxious, exhausted, and traumatised.

All except Spock, that is. She leaned into me and whimpered. While the rest of us had been run ragged by the constant demands of the trelane, Spock adored them. She'd spent the journey romping, playing, licking, and wrestling with the bastards. She actually *missed* them.

BB pulled herself up to her full height and clicked her beak. 'Well, we'd better get on with the clean-up. Lord knows we've got our work cut out for us.'

Bexley's nostrils flared and Henry vented a pungent gas.

'I, er, have an idea.' I had to stave off the helplessness. 'The mess will still be there in a few hours, right? So why don't we take a break? Wind down.'

Bexley looked at me funny, squinting her eyes. 'You're not going to make us play Lizard in the Basement again, are you?'

I shook my head. 'It's called Dungeons and Dragons.'

Bexley tapped her hooves in the air. 'Sorry, yeah. That's the one. Basements and Lizards. I don't think it translates well.'

Our personal AIs were brilliant, providing real-time translation so we could all communicate with relative ease. It wasn't just about differing languages. Spock's communication worked mostly based on scent. Bexley couldn't hear BB's vocal register at all. Aurora was a cloud of sentient gas – I didn't even know *how* she communicated.

And then there was the fact that we all came from different species on our own worlds with diverse mythologies and experiences and physiologies and, well, some things just didn't translate.

Darmok and Jalad were right about everything. 'Actually, I've come up with something new. An idea I've been playing with.'

Back on Earth – before I was kidnapped by confused bounty hunters – I'd played so many different RPGs. One of my favourites was about a group of freelancers on a space-ship who took on all sorts of jobs. But now Stardust Wake had somehow become my life.

The *Teapot* crew were down with the idea of games – even role-playing ones. But D&D had been a massive flop. The creatures, powers, and mythologies just hadn't translated. And, quite frankly, I winced every time I remembered saying the paladin was atop her noble steed.

I'd considered getting them to give Stardust Wake a try – but it'd be like asking a group of my fellow early twenty-first-century humans to play a game about getting up in the morning, grabbing a coffee, and going to the office.

Being so jaded had almost killed my love of gaming. But in the end, I flipped my ennui on its head and turned my life before the *Teapot* into an RPG.

———

'So,' I said when we were all seated. 'Over the past few weeks —'

Bexley gently nudged me in the ribs. 'While you were hiding in the bathroom.'

I arched an eyebrow. 'Sure, yes. This is a game I devised while hiding in the bathroom.' I tried to glare at her – but I couldn't help cracking a grin.

'I think it's safe to say we all did our fair share of hiding from the frocking trelane.'

I blinked, checking my watch to be sure it really said: HENRY SPEAKING.

'Wow, Henry. Thank you.' I was pretty sure she'd never come to my defence before.

Henry rolled away from me. 'Yeah, well, the cupping

trelane made even you look civilised and refined by comparison.'

'Whatever.'

Different species' imaginations worked in different ways. But my new game was grounded in our reality. It was built on things we all shared: contract work, difficulty in communication, and that nigh-universal frustration when customers just wouldn't tell you what they wanted.

The game progressed well over the next two hours. But then, as project master, I tossed a spanner into the works: scope creep. As the players considered how to adapt their strategies, I gazed out the mess hall's massive window at the distant stars. We were in warp, which always seemed to blur their edges. In the corner of the room, there stood an array of plants we'd worked together to establish – just one of the changes we'd made in the months since Bexley bought the *Teapot* from our former captors.

'I don't see how it's a sudden request,' said Bexley in character as the customer. 'The tool can't possibly manage our inventory if it doesn't also manage sales.' Her eyes locked onto Aurora, who was playing the project manager.

Aurora's rainbow receded as indigo came to the forefront. Two weeks ago, I wouldn't have been able to tell you what that colour meant – but I'd seen enough of it in recent days to recognise it as irritation. 'Difficult. You hired us to build an inventory management tool, not a sales tool. We've already used most of the allotted development time.'

Despite the annoyance indicated by Aurora's colouring, her voice came through in the same smooth, buttery tones as always. 'There will be an extra charge for this. But what does the developer think? How much extra work are we talking? Can it be done within the agreed schedule or do we need to delay?'

BB clucked and then hummed, a talon tapping anxiously against the table. 'I roll the dice now, yes?'

I tapped my fists in the air. Somewhere along the way, I'd fallen into the habit of using Bexley's version of nodding.

She picked up the plastic icosahedron and sent it clattering against the tabletop. When it stopped moving, she peered over, her bright yellow wings ruffling as she considered her response. 'Well, er ... you see ... the central framework is relatively stable, so adding an inventory module is doable. But the team we outsourced the UI to is already three days overdue. We're definitely going to need at least a few more weeks to build the new code.'

Aurora hummed as she studied her screen.

For a moment, there was silence, a question unasked ... before Henry flapped a brush of some sort. 'I could build your parking code in about nine minutes flat.'

I pinched the bridge of my nose. 'This isn't real life, Henry. It's a game. You're not the developer – you're QA.'

Henry wheeled in a tight circle, stopping to wave her little brush in my face. 'Excuse me. I do actually know that. This is me getting into character. My character took this job in QA because she was desperate after she lost her last job due to downsizing. Then her ex-spouse ran off with the nanny. Now she's got a litter of seventeen children to look after and no child support coming in.'

'I don't think —' I began.

But Henry wasn't done. She held up that same brush in a sort of stop or wait gesture. 'She wants to be an opera singer. Her ex always promised to support her, so she's doubly bitter – having been let go from a job she loved and unable to pursue her dreams. Funnily enough, she doesn't actually miss her snake of an ex – but she does miss the nanny. So, yes, she says she could build the code faster. And she doesn't think very highly of BB's dev team. So she's definitely going to need some extra time to test the code they send.'

I bit my lips to keep from chuckling.

'There you go, Bexley,' Aurora said. 'Three extra weeks – two for dev and one for QA. How's that?'

'Excellent!' I thumped the table cheerfully.

Spock, who'd been snoozing under the table, awoke with a start and banged her head. 'Ow. Bad table.'

She climbed onto the sofa with me. When she had turned three times in a circle, she lay down and went back to sleep. I ran my hand over her thick fur, scratching behind her ears.

Still, the players had finally come to an agreement on what their next actions would be.

I tapped a few keys on my phone. 'Okay, Bexley, make a roll on the timeframe table to see how urgent your need for the new software module is. Aurora, good job with the role play, but I need you to —'

Holly interrupted me. 'You have a message from the Office of the Galactic Minister for Refugees. Would you like to hear it now?'

'I what?'

A quick glance around the room told me the others were receiving the same news and were equally surprised.

'You have a message from the Office of the Galactic Minister for Refugees. Would you like to hear it now?'

I felt my pulse race as a wave of dizziness washed over me. Which was silly. It wasn't about me. I had every right to exist in the galaxy. I paid my citizenship fees and taxes. It wasn't like I was an illegal immigrant in the galaxy I was born in – not that there was any such thing out here in space. 'Yeah, play it please, Holly.'

A soft voice spoke in my ear. 'This message is being broadcast to all ships in the delta quadrant. The Galactic

Minister for Refugees requests your assistance on an urgent mission. If you have capacity to take on passengers and are within about four days' travel of the co-ordinates attached to this message, please join the minister for a Q&A session tomorrow morning. This is a paid mission. The time and dial-in details for the meeting are attached to this message. We hope to see you there. Message ends.'

Bexley clapped. 'Ooh! A job for the Galactic Union. How exciting! And for the refugee ministry at that. I wonder what it could be? It sounds like it involves transporting people – presumably refugees. Well, I guess we'd better get back to work, cleaning this place up.'

2 / UNINTENDED COIFFURE

As I got dressed the next morning, I asked, 'Holly, I don't actually know anything about the Galactic Central Government. Can you give me a potted version of how they work, so I'm not totally unprepared, please? I don't want to make an arse of myself. I haven't got the patience or energy for a big lecture – just the quick and dirty overview.'

'The Galactic Central Government serves as a supraplanetary body,' replied the disembodied voice in my ear, 'enhancing rather than replacing local governments. Its purpose is to support common interests – mainly trade – as well as to uphold peace and person rights. Citizens of the galaxy have freedom to live, work, and study on any member planet.'

That explanation brought an involuntary scoff from me as Spock and I exited our room. 'All right, so it's the EU. Well, the GU, I suppose. What are person rights?'

'There are thirty fundamental statements in the GU's person rights charter. Number one: all sapient beings have the right to life. Number two: all sapients are free and equal.

Number three: no person or group shall be held in slavery. Number four: discrimination on any basis—'

I stepped into the lift. 'Okay, okay. I got you. That's enough. Top deck, please. Is there anything else I need to know?'

'Given that the meeting has been called by the GU's Minister for Refugees, it's likely that this job will pertain to the safety and security of people in crisis.'

'Thanks.' I yawned noisily as I exited the lift. We'd all worked as late into the night as we could manage. BB had crashed out first. Her species, the peri, needed twelve straight hours of sleep a night or they got seriously cranky. I'd stayed up much later than I normally would – but I'd managed to catch about four hours.

The holo-call would bring us right into the room with the meeting organisers, so it wouldn't do for us to be sitting in a room with broken furniture and tufts of slime-coated fur on every surface. We'd banned the trelane from the bridge deck – including Ten Backwards, our main meeting space – but those bastards got everywhere. I stifled another yawn.

'Morning, Lem,' said Aurora when I ducked through the meeting room door. 'I thought you might appreciate a cup of tea. And I've brought Spock's breakfast.'

I rubbed sleep gunk from my eyes. 'Oh, bless you. You're a saint.' Once I'd set Spock's food on the floor, I picked up my mug of colourless *tea* and breathed the sweet, life-giving vapours. I'd grab a mug of stimulant later. For now, the flavour profile and aromas still provided a psychosomatic pick-me-up. I dropped onto one of the sofas.

A moment later, Henry and Bexley came into view.

A gasp escaped my lips before I could stop myself. 'Bexley!'

She reached a hoof to her mane – her glorious, wavy

blond mane. It hung down her back past her hips. Or at least it had until some four hours ago. Now it ended in a choppy, uneven line just above her shoulders.

'Um, yeah.' She snorted. 'I... That is...' She stopped speaking. In the three months I'd known her, Bexley was never short of words. Never. Just didn't happen. She sank heavily into a chair and dropped her head onto the table with a dull thud.

Henry flipped out an implement I didn't think I'd seen her sporting before. My suspicions were confirmed when she snipped violently with what turned out to be a pair of scissors. 'Your pal here leant in something while we were cleaning out the cells.'

The *Teapot*'s former prison cells had been converted into sleeping quarters for our guests.

'Oh no,' I said. Spock finished her breakfast and curled up under the table. Reaching a hand out to stroke Bexley's back, I discovered that several patches of the fur on her back had been shaved as well. 'What was it? What happened?'

Beneath my hand, I could feel Bexley heave a shudder. Aurora swept over and joined me in trying to comfort her – she didn't seem surprised, though. The edges of Aurora's form trickled through Bexley's mane.

'I don't know.' If translations still sounded from my watch, I'd have missed Bexley's reply. The words were barely a whisper. But I'd recently added an earpiece.

Aurora's dominant colours were red and royal blue, which I was pretty sure indicated a combination of sadness and anxiety. 'I don't know what the substance was, but as soon as she touched it, Bexley's hair and fur began to dissolve. Henry cut it off to stop it from spreading. Fortunately, she didn't get much on her skin. We even dragged my lovely spouse out of bed in the middle of the night to check her over.'

'Oh no, I'm so sorry, mate. I'm just glad you weren't hurt.'

Aurora pointed towards another mug on the table. 'Lem, if you'd be so kind. That mug is Bexley's favourite – hot apple juice. I thought it might ... help.'

I took the mug and put it in front of Bexley. She sniffed the air, then raised her head slightly, and pulled the mug towards herself.

Just then, the holo-feed kicked in and we found ourselves facing two people. It looked like they were in the room with us – if the room had three separate interior designers who'd disagreed on everything.

Ten Backwards was like some sort of minimalist but comfortable Scandi-style living room. Ahead and to my left, a bird-person – a peri, I thought – stood in a leafy, green space. And to her right sat a ... sort of fur-covered shape. With a beak. And three eyes. The furry person sat in the most disorganised, chaotic, cluttered space imaginable. Just looking at it made me want to sneeze.

'Good morning,' said the peri. 'Thank you for taking this meeting on such short notice. I am the GU Minister for Refugees and I am joined this morning by the programme manager who has been selected to oversee the evacuation of a populated planet.'

In space, no one can hear you introduce yourself.

Well, that is to say, names didn't translate. Sometimes they comprised noises another species couldn't make or couldn't hear. Other times they had meanings that were sort of like inside jokes shared by a whole culture or planet. So the universal translator didn't try and most people didn't bother. Instead, people assigned names of their choosing to everyone they met. Or let their AIs choose for them.

Hence, people introduced themselves and one another using job titles or by describing how they were connected.

That reminded me... The programme manager looked like someone who would solve minor problems by turning them into major disasters. I decided to call her Rincewind – *no, Rincy*. I was probably judging her too harshly – I blamed my sleep-deprived state.

'Five days from now,' the government minister said, 'an asteroid of significant mass will collide with the planet. The colonists need to be evacuated safely. This region of space isn't well travelled, so it's fortuitous we had a GU employee who happened to be in the vicinity of the planet when we first learnt of the impending disaster.'

The minister turned to Rincy, who lifted three arms – two in the usual place and one in the centre of her chest. With one arm, she rustled a stack of papers. The other two scratched her head. 'Yes, um. Thank you, Minister.'

She rocked back on her chair – and promptly fell over, taking an entire shelf of assorted stuff down with her. Reminding myself she wasn't really here, I refrained from leaping to her assistance. Instead, I glanced at my friends while we waited for Rincy to recover herself.

I could almost hear Henry rolling her eyes. Metaphorically, at any rate. Bexley was staring dead ahead, her eyes unfocused. I was pretty sure she was asleep. Aurora glowed mostly yellow.

Rincy spent several seconds trying to rearrange the shelf and its contents, before giving up and dumping everything on the desk in front of herself. A box or device of some sort slid across the table towards me. I flinched, but it winked out of view before it could hit me.

With her various hands, Rincy smoothed her fur. 'Sorry, er, as I was saying, we're calling on all available ships that have any spare capacity to make for the planet without delay. The population is approximately four thousand. Our plan is to transport them to Phoebe station where they will remain while the minister and her team work to find them a new home.'

She jerked one of her limbs, knocking the pile of stuff off her table again. While she attempted to collect it, the room expanded again as someone else joined the virtual call. I gasped as a wall of water appeared on my right. Reminding myself it was only a hologram, I forced myself to breathe.

'If I may be so bold,' proclaimed a sing-songy voice that my watch identified as belonging to Gracie, who I assumed was the whale-esque person in the water tank. She flapped her – I wasn't sure if they were legs or flippers. If the scale of the display was one to one, she was probably at least double the mass of a human. She didn't have a face – at least not one I could identify. 'Why is this being done at the last minute? These plans should have been set in motion years ago.'

Rincy was outside the holo-camera's range, doing who knew what. *How is this person in charge of a mission of this scale?*

The government minister clucked. 'Yes, thank you, Captain Gracie. That's an excellent question. One I asked the local government myself, I assure you. However, it seems that they were unaware of the impending disaster.'

'Unaware?' roared Gracie. 'How could they have been unaware? This asteroid should have been visible to them for quite some time.'

The minister lifted a little taloned hand to her beak and stroked it. 'Again, I raised these points myself. However, it seems that the scientists were deemed to be speaking from a politically unfashionable perspective. As such, their warnings were viewed as metaphorical rather than literal.'

The silence that followed lingered just long enough to be uncomfortable.

Gracie's voice was still a song, but the pitch and tempo both increased. 'So now we've all got to drop what we're doing and run to their aid – all because the people decided they'd had enough of experts? Is that what you're telling us, Minister?'

Rincy popped back up and spoke smoothly. 'This isn't charity. You will be compensated for your efforts. Nor are you being ordered to do anything. We're *requesting* all ships in the sector to join us in this urgent rescue mission. But no one is forcing anyone to do anything.'

Rincy waved an arm, nearly sending the carefully rebuilt stack of junk flying again, but another of her arms caught it before it tumbled off the edge of the table. 'We hope you'll join us. The more of you participate, the easier the work will be – but we don't *need* everyone —'

'Then you can count the *Pequod* out!' Gracie disappeared from the meeting room without further ado.

The minister clicked her beak. 'The loss of the *Pequod* to the mission is … unfortunate. Gracie's ship was one of the largest. They have capacity for over a thousand people. Without them, if we're to have any hope of saving the colonists, we'll need almost all of you to join us. As Rincy says, no one will be compelled. But we do hope you'll agree to take this job.'

Bexley sat bolt upright for the first time since she'd taken her seat. 'Can I ask a question, please?'

Rincy sort of waddled in place. 'Ah, yes. I believe we have a question from the crew of the *Teapot*. Captain Bexley, please go ahead.'

Bexley ran her hooves over her forelock, forcing it down over her long equine nose. 'Um, hi. Good morning, everybody.' She'd once confided to me that she used her forelock to cover the remnants of a unicorn horn. She was horrifically embarrassed about it. Something about her people seeing unicorns as animals rather than people – lesser beings. It didn't make sense to me – Bexley was the best person I knew. *How could anyone think she's just an animal?* 'Thanks for inviting us to join you in this mission. I hope I can speak for my crew when I say we're in – though we still need to vote, of course.'

I groaned inwardly. We needed a break after what we'd gone through with the trelane. But I understood.

'But, um,' Bexley continued. 'In order for us to calculate how many people we can accommodate, we'll need the specs of the local species as well as their cargo. I mean, they could be sort of anywhere between a tribble and an aurochs and while we can definitely accommodate some people of either size, it would really help us … well, um … if you could tell us how big they are.'

Rincy was rocking her head from side to side slightly. 'Thank you, Bexley. Er, you should have received the specs already. But I can get someone to send them to you again if you need.'

My watch buzzed and I glanced down at it: SHE DEFINITELY DIDN'T.

Bexley tapped her hooves softly on the table in front of herself. 'Yes, please send them. If you don't mind.'

'Lem,' Holly interrupted, 'do you have a designation for the planet to be evacuated?'

My right eyelid started twitching. 'I don't know, Holly,' I whispered. 'Call it Dave.' It was the first name that came to mind.

Whatever. Maybe one day I'd get the hang of naming people and species and planets – but that day wasn't today.

'Right,' said Rincy. 'Anyone else need reminding of the specs again?' She paused so the other ships could reply. 'Ah, yes. That's er… That's quite a few of you, actually. Maybe there's something wrong with my email.' She picked something up off the table in front of her. 'I'll just … hang on…'

The government minister was scratching her head again, feathers turning in every direction as she twirled her talons through them. 'I'll have my team send the specs to everyone on this call as soon as we're done. As I mentioned, though, without the *Pequod* and her considerable resources, we really are counting on all of you to help out with this evacuation. I must stress how dire the need is. No one will be forced to do anything they're not comfortable with. However, these people will die if we do not remove them from the planet this week.'

3 / ACCIDENTAL PORN
INCURSION

After the meeting, Henry went up to the bridge and the rest of us gathered in the mess for breakfast. BB – who had only just woken up – joined us as we were finishing. Once all the dishes were cleared away, we sat back down to strategise our part in the rescue mission.

We reviewed the specs the minister had sent us – including photos. The residents of planet Dave looked sort of cat-like but with six limbs: four legs and two arms. They had similar mass to humans, but because they stood on four legs, they were shorter and took up more space.

Henry rolled into the room. 'I've set a course for the Grand Bazaar. It's the nearest station where we can refuel and load up on supplies.' She extended what looked like a small plunger, making her look a bit dalek-y. 'Unfortunately, it will take us six hours in the wrong direction, but we can't go into this mission without replenishing our stocks.'

Bexley looked up from her third mug of hot apple juice, her features still blank and her eyes dull. 'Thanks, Henry.'

I tapped my lip, thinking things through as I spoke. 'Based on what Rincy said, it sounds like there could be an issue evacuating all the plenties if any of the other ships decide not to participate. I think we should calculate how many of them we can comfortably accommodate but also how many we can feasibly squeeze in if it comes down to it. And we ought to stock up based on the latter figure.'

Henry wheeled in a tight circle. 'What did you think we were going to do? Just stick a finger in the air and guess? Not that I even have fingers.'

Spock, who'd been curled up in a ball, shifted positions to stretch out. Bexley pulled her legs up under herself on the sofa to accommodate Spock.

'I must say, I agree with that plan,' said Aurora, glowing turquoise. 'As much as I don't relish the thought of sharing our space again for a while, we can't leave people to die just because they're being too wilfully stupid to listen to their own scientists.'

BB sat on her perch in the corner, daintily pecking at her food. 'Did the *Pequod*'s captain really decline to join because of the government's ignorance?'

I nodded and Bexley tapped her hooves. 'Yep,' we replied in unison.

'Puffer duckers,' unswore Henry.

BB fluttered her feathers anxiously. 'She does have a point. The plenties are in this mess through their own negligence.'

Bexley sat upright and looked alert for the first time all morning. 'Hey now. That's not fair. What if there's more we don't know? I mean, who'd actually choose death by asteroid? And anyways, we can't doom thousands of people because some of them chose ignorance over taking responsibility. The planet's destruction isn't even their fault. When faced with overwhelming news, some people just can't cope. Rather than take charge and deal with the crisis, sometimes it's easier to bury your head in the sand. Like, when I was just a foal, one of my dads was killed in a bizarre gardening accident. I was only six and I couldn't deal, so I built up this story that she'd gone away on a—'

Bexley ran her hooves through her short, uneven mane. 'Um, anyways. We still have a duty to rescue these people.'

I reached out to stroke her back gently. 'Of course we will.'

Aurora shifted to lemon yellow – a colour I was pretty sure indicated embarrassment – and floated gracefully towards her spouse. 'I'm sure BB didn't intend for us to follow Gracie.'

'Of course not.' BB plucked at her chest feathers with her beak. 'I was simply expressing sympathy with *why* Gracie chose to leave. I wasn't suggesting we should do likewise. It's possible to understand why she made the decision she did without agreeing she was right to do so. I would never...' She looked around the room. 'Genuinely, I wouldn't.'

———

It took us a day and a half to get to Dave. We could have got there quicker but the trip to Grand Bazaar station slowed us down. Even still, we were the first to arrive. After Rincy, that is. Her ship – which was shaped like an otter – had arrived shortly after the meeting with the minister.

She invited us to come aboard to take part in the planning stage of the mission. We decided that Aurora and BB would remain on the *Teapot* and the rest of us would join Rincy on her ship for the meeting.

'Welcome, welcome,' Rincy said as we stepped from our ship onto hers. In person, she looked kind of like a platypus.

'I suppose we should get the introductions out of the way first. I believe you're the captain?'

Bexley tilted her head to one side and then the other. 'Well, technically. I suppose that's what it lists on the *Teapot*'s registration. But really we operate as more of an autonomous collective. Mainly, I serve as the mechanic. This is our pilot. She's also handy with computers. And finally our … um … operations organiser,' she said, indicating Henry and me, respectively. 'Do you have a meeting space we can use?'

We were still standing in the docking bay of Rincy's strange ship. Though I suppose given that our ship looked like an actual teapot, *strange* may not have meant much.

Rincy's ship was furry – inside and out. *Why would a spaceship be furry?* As we walked through her corridors, I reached out a hand to touch the wall – but drew back when something on it moved.

Rincy led us down a dimly lit corridor crowded with boxes and assorted equipment to a flight of stairs. Everything was coated in a thick layer of dust. Sticky dust. I gave a silent thanks for BB's powerful antihistamines. They were probably the only reason I wasn't having an asthma attack.

Bexley climbed a few steps before turning back. 'Oh.'

I followed her eyes. Henry stood at the bottom of the steps.

'Stairs…' I began.

Henry extended and retracted several stabby-looking implements. 'Yes, meatsacks. Frolicking stairs.'

I looked around for something that looked like a ramp – or even something that could be used as one. There was plenty of … stuff. But nothing that looked flat enough.

Rincy climbed back down the steps. 'Oh, I see. It's no problem. I can carry you.' She extended several of her arms towards Henry – who slapped what looked like a paper fan at her. 'Or not. Er…'

Seriously, how is she in charge of this mission?

'I'll just go back to my ship, shall I? Don't worry, these ugly bags of mostly water can catch me up on things later.' Henry rolled back a bit. 'What kind of bollarding parkas put stairs in a carping spaceship?'

I shrugged. 'Er, Rincy, if you don't have an accessible meeting space, may I suggest we meet aboard the *Teapot*?' To be honest, I didn't relish the idea of sitting on her furniture anyway. Everything we'd seen of her ship was coated in dust.

'Oh, um, yeah, actually…' Bexley pushed her forelock down over her long nose. 'We've got a meeting room we could use.'

'Oh, I'm sure that's not nec—' Rincy's words were cut off as she stumbled over a thing that looked like a stationary tricycle. 'Well, actually, maybe that's not a terrible idea. I love my ship – but it doesn't have a space big enough for all four of us. Maybe this wasn't the best plan.'

Bexley and I helped Rincy to her feet. Her shaggy fur was silkier than I had expected. And stickier. Like satin dipped in honey. I tried to be subtle as I wiped my hands on my trousers.

Rincy turned to head back up the stairs, her tail nearly knocking Bexley over as she did so. 'No problem. I'll grab my tablet and then I'll join you.' Her feet made a claggy slapping sound on the stairs as she disappeared from view.

I made to lean on the wall, then thought better of it. 'Is she, er… Are we expecting her back in a few seconds or should we wait on the *Teapot*?'

'If I stand still any longer,' said Henry, 'I'll probably end up glued to the decking floor.'

Bexley leaned forwards and sniffed at something that

looked like a cross between a toilet and a kitchen mixer. 'Let's head back. She'll ping us when she's ready.'

————

Half an hour later, we gathered on the top deck of the *Teapot* in Ten Backwards. The clear dome above us was filled with a view of the planet below. Above. Whatever – up and down are hard in space.

When we were kidnapped by the bunnyboos, the *Teapot* was their ship. We'd made a few significant changes after Bexley bought it. According to Aurora, the bunnyboos had never done much with this amazing space, using it mainly for storage. But when Bexley bought the ship, we'd turned it into an extra lounge area. And with the out-of-this-world view and the sleek new mod cons, it was great for showing off.

Spock was lying on the floor licking her pink plush brain squeaky toy when we heard the lift doors open on the bridge.

Bexley's voice reached us before she did. 'So, anyways, then I said to her, "I can't believe you didn't tell me she was here." Because obviously, if I'd known it was her, I never would have suggested *that*.'

'Oh my gosh,' said Rincy as they came around the ship's central column into view. 'That's fantastic.'

The moment they appeared in the doorway, Spock charged over, jumped up, and put her paws on Rincy, bowling her over. She covered her with sloppy kisses. 'Pretty friend!'

I pulled Spock off. 'No! Off. Bad girl.' I reached out a hand to help Rincy up, but she waved me away. 'I'm so sorry. She doesn't normally do anything like that.'

Spock sat down by my side, but continued to wag her tail and stare at Rincy.

Rincy chuckled and hauled herself to her feet. 'Well, you certainly are friendly, aren't you?'

'Pretty friend,' repeated Spock. 'Smell nice.' She nosed forwards again, still trying to lick Rincy.

'I'm so sorry.' My cheeks were burning. 'Spock, you mustn't bother Rincy. We're here to work, not to play.'

Rincy bent down and gave Spock a cuddle, the furry pair of them licking and grooming one another. The mutual snuggling carried on for a bit.

I looked at Bexley. Bexley looked at me. We both looked at Henry.

After a few moments, Rincy stood back up. 'Oh, hello. The gang's all here, I see. Hi, everyone. Sorry about the delay. I went up to my office to fetch my tablet to show you the plans, but then there was a message from two more ships that will be arriving in the next few hours. Still, I suppose it's best for us to get stuck in right away.'

Henry muttered something ... I thought I caught the word 'stuck'.

From her perch across from me, BB lifted her wings in greeting. 'Good morning, Rincy. I'll be glad to offer my assistance as a multi-species medic. I attended the galaxy-renowned medical school on Quoth and gained some notoriety for my skill in treating diverse species. And this is my spouse.'

Aurora let the edges of her shapeless, rainbow-hued form blur into BB's shoulders. 'Thank you so much for joining us, Rincy. I provide domestic support on the *Teapot* – cooking, cleaning, inventory management. And I'm not afraid of a bit of hard work.'

Spock looked up from her spot on the floor. 'Spock good girl,' she said before curling her head into her paws and returning to sleep.

'Spock also serves as our physical security officer,' said Bexley. 'And the rest of us you know.'

Rincy rolled her shoulders, muscles rippling beneath her fur. 'Right, thank you, everyone. I suppose it's best if we get straight to business. I've brought my tablet so I can show you the plans I've put together. Have you got a holo I can connect to?'

'Pinging you the details now,' replied Henry.

'Excellent.' Rincy fumbled with her tablet for a few seconds as Henry switched the projector on. An animated cartoon creature that looked like a velvet gecko – the 3D logo for the software company – appeared in the room. Standing about a metre in height, it twirled gracefully on its axis as Rincy scrabbled to set things up.

The first time that logo had appeared in the room, Spock had tried to eat it. Poor doggo, she was so confused when her jaws clamped down over nothing.

'Okay, okay,' said Rincy, spinning to face the hologram. She clicked a few more buttons and…

BB squawked.

'Oh, dear me.' Aurora glowed yellow – her version of blushing.

Bexley sidled towards the grunting, groaning, squealing figures who'd appeared in the middle of the room. She tipped herself upside down, trying to get a better view.

My cheeks burned. I tried to look away, but I was transfixed. The rutting people – I thought there were three of them, but I wasn't entirely sure… The noises they made were unambiguous. Limbs and tentacles squirmed and writhed. Maybe one of the people was the same species as Rincy.

Do not glance over at her. Don't turn your head, Lem. Do not look at her.

Another one appeared to have scales. But there were

feathers in the mix too. I wasn't sure if one of the, er, lovers *had* feathers – maybe she was just wearing them.

Bexley was still bent over, inspecting the action up close and personal. 'Is this *Octopussy*? I haven't seen it yet. It came out a couple of weeks back, right? Like, I ordered it ages ago, but it's been on back order since— Um, sorry. Um…'

Rincy finally seemed to notice the porn. 'Oh, er… Sorry. This isn't what I was trying to put up on the display.' *Well, obviously.* She began touching buttons on her tablet. 'How do I stop it?' She swiped left and right … then paused to appreciate the action for a bit.

'Oh, for the love of cat,' said Henry. The melodramatic moaning and screaming ceased and the figures vanished. A grabby tool extended on a flexible cord, snatching the tablet from Rincy's hands. When Henry had retracted it halfway back to her formless cylinder, she paused. 'May I?' Her voice was dry – it probably sounded polite to someone who didn't know her well.

Rincy looked towards Henry. 'Of course. Sorry about that. I forgot to close the file I was watching. Er, can you access a file called…' Her middle arm reached up and scratched her head. 'I think it was called "Dave rescue plan" or maybe "evacuation mission" or something like that. I really should make a note of these things.' She waved her arms around in a sort of helpless gesture. 'I suppose I probably did. In the file, I mean.'

I pinched the bridge of my nose as a scaled-down version of the planet Dave popped into existence in the middle of the room, spinning leisurely. Sparkly turquoise clouds floated above a planet that showed blue seas and land masses that ranged from orange to purple – just like the view out of the clear dome above us.

'Ah, excellent,' said Rincy. 'Thank you, Henry. This is the

planet Dave.' She waddled across the floor to the model. 'The main settlement is...' One of her webbed hands meandered over the surface as she searched.

BB was still preening her feathers and generally looking awkward – her species was notoriously prudish. Even more so than humans. Well, even more than this admittedly also prudish human. She stepped gingerly down off her perch and walked towards the centre of the room. One of the little hands under her wings peeked out and pointed to a green X on the surface of the planet. 'Is this it?'

BB followed the mark with her talon as the miniature planet revolved. Rincy shuffled to where BB pointed. 'Ah, yes. This is the plentitudian city. The plan' – she clicked a button on her tablet – 'is this.'

At least a dozen ships appeared in orbit around planet Dave – including one dayglo pink teapot. Two small turquoise cubes lifted off from the surface, just next to the X. They increased in size as they approached the orbiting ships. A moment later, the cubes were swallowed up by a large ship that looked like a fried egg.

Rincy pointed at the egg-ship. 'As you can see, the *Egg* is a cargo ship. It's equipped with two ground-to-orbit vehicles for moving up to seventy-two people at a time. From the *Egg*, they'll transfer to the various ships we have arriving in the next three days.'

As a project manager, this was the sort of crap I lived for. I could see a thousand different ways it could all go spectacularly wrong if the details weren't carefully anticipated. 'How is the evacuation being organised?'

Rincy's beak – or was it more of a bill? – hung open for a moment. She pointed at the little flying cubes. 'The ground-to-orbit vehicles. The residents will use the ground-to-orbit vehicles.'

I pursed my lips. 'Okay, but what I mean is how long does each round trip take? And how much time is needed for loading and unloading? How will the plenties know where and when to catch the right transport? Who decides who travels on which ship? Do they have any special require-ments? How much stuff is each person allowed to bring? Are there any pets?' I bit back several more questions – I could do this all day.

Rincy looked like she was about to argue, then closed her bill. She stabbed a hand in my direction. 'Those are excellent questions. I like you, Lem. You seem like you know about managing a mission of this scale. I'll admit I'm in a bit over my head – I was thrust into this role because I was in the right place at the right time.' She ran a webbed finger down the length of her bill. 'Or the wrong place at the wrong time. I don't know if you're aware of this – but I'm not actually a project manager.'

No kidding.

She waved her arms around and for the first time, I spotted a fourth one in the middle of her back. 'I'd like you to accompany me to meet with the colony's leader this afternoon to co-ordinate the evacuation. Bexley, would you be willing to join us as well?'

4 / CATS WILL BE CATS

Just over four hours later, I was 'enjoying' a transporter journey – a seemingly endless thrill-ride on a rollercoaster-cum-sensory-deprivation-chamber. The pod was just large enough for me. It was lined with a squishy gel to protect me from damage. I couldn't see out and the only sounds were transmitted through my earpiece.

At length, I felt the cessation of motion that told me I was presumably at my destination. Transporter pods rarely go to the wrong place or stop in the middle of nowhere – or so they tell me.

When Holly assured me it was safe to do so, I checked that my nose prongs were in place and stepped out of the pod. The planet's atmosphere had a lower percentage of oxygen than Earth did. Not by much. It was within the tolerability limits of the other *Teapot* crew members, but Spock and I had to wear little devices – like nasal cannulas – blowing air at us to make sure we got sufficient oxygen.

The gravity here was lighter than on Earth as well. The *Teapot*'s gravity was similar to what I was used to but this made me feel like I was floating. As I headed for Spock's pod,

I had a chance to look around. We'd landed in a pod-park station, which was paved in bright purple concrete.

Above us, the sky was more turquoise than blue. There was a green space beyond the edges of the lot – well, not *green*. The dominant colour was orange. A public park, maybe? Orange grass covered the ground and there were trees with grey trunks and enormous gold leaves. Where Earth trees might have flowers or fruit, these ones had bubbles in a whole rainbow of colours. On the whole, it was both like Earth and not like it at all.

We seemed to be at the edge of a city. I considered what to call it. Purris? Kittyminster? Mew York? No, *Catford*!

I released Spock from her pod. After covering me in excited kisses, she bounded along to Bexley's pod where we waited for her. The areion, Bexley's species, always lost consciousness in transport. To be honest, I was jealous. I'd love to mentally skip over the harrowing voyage.

After a moment, Bexley leapt out. As always, she bolted into the open space beyond the pods and danced in circles around us for a full minute, neighing and braying. 'Whoa, that was a heck of a wild rush! It used to hit me like that when I was a foal, but I don't think I've had that strong of a reaction since —'

Whatever she was going to say next was drowned out by Spock's frantic barking. I had brought a lead but hadn't yet put it on her. Ever since we got the translators that enabled us to communicate directly, it felt cruel to put her on a leash. As she charged towards the group of plenties at the edge of the park, I discovered my mistake.

Most of the people scattered and ran, but one raced up into one of the orange bubble trees.

'Spock, no,' I shouted in my very best authoritative voice as I scrambled to close the distance between us.

Raising my voice didn't help. Spock was on her hind legs, barking furiously, pounding on the tree. The cat-like person hissed at Spock and swatted down at her. Long claws extended from dainty lime-green paws.

Holly normally translated everything Spock said. But there was nothing this time. Just pure animal instinct.

I caught up with her and snapped the lead onto her collar. 'Spock, down.'

She resisted me. Spock could be stubborn – but I was more so.

After an endless moment she sat down on her haunches, still panting heavily. 'Tasty kitty.' She glared at the green-spotted plenti.

The muscles along my jaw clenched up. 'No! This is a diplomatic mission. You are not going to ruin it. If you can't behave, you'll go back to the *Teapot*.'

She glanced at me before returning her focus to the plenti. 'Not eat tasty kitty?'

'We're here to help these people. Not eat them. If you try to eat one more person on this planet, you'll spend the whole week in the ship. No ... eating ... anyone.'

The tips of Spock's ears dipped forwards.

I looked up to see that Bexley had coaxed the plenti down from the tree. Before I could apologise, she bolted away.

While most of the plenties were keeping their distance, one made straight towards us. She was pure white in colour, though I'd seen a wide variety of different hues already. They looked sort of like cat-centaurs.

I fastened Spock's lead to my waist. No possibility of escape for her. 'I'm so sorry about that.'

Bexley pulled her lips back from her big teeth. 'Maybe Spock should go back to the *Teapot* for today, Lem. I love her and all. But I don't think we're in any danger here. Well, I mean, we're obviously in danger – there's a great big old asteroid heading straight for us and we wouldn't want to find ourselves stuck on the planet when it arrives. But there's no *immediate* risk – so her services aren't needed right now.'

'Yeah, you're right.' I nodded and turned back to Spock. 'Sorry, boo. It's not okay to eat the people we're here to help. You go back up to the ship. Aurora will make you some treats, okay? Everything will be fine.'

Spock's tail fell and she turned her head up to look at me. 'Spock bad girl?'

I couldn't resist that face. I never could. 'You're a very good girl – usually. But you mustn't eat the plenties.'

'Spock sorry.'

I stroked her fur. 'It's okay, mate. You just get in the pod. Aurora will look after you.' I patted the pod. 'Come on, in you go.'

She gave me a final dejected glance and padded in. I did up her seatbelt and checked it, then stroked her head. 'That's my girl. I love you, Spock. I'll see you in a few hours.'

I closed the pod and called Aurora to let her know what was happening. After a quick chat with her, I headed back to where Bexley waited near the bright white plenti. The latter used a single dangerous-looking claw to tap and swipe on her phone. She wasn't looking at Bexley or me. If anything, I'd say she looked bored.

'Hey, Lem,' said Bexley. 'This is the prime minister's assistant. I've apologised on behalf of Spock and told her how sorry we all are for the misunderstanding.' She turned back to the plenti. 'We had no idea she would respond that way to anyone. I've certainly never seen her do that before. Spock is one of our most valued crew members and a good friend, actually. I mean, obviously all our crew is valued, but—'

I looked away as an image of Spock barking at neighbourhood cats danced through my mind. My face warmed.

The cat-person licked a paw and rubbed her face with it. 'No bother. I feel like chasing the protesters up a tree most days too.'

Protesters?

'Hello,' called Rincy as she waddled over to join us. I hadn't even noticed her pod land.

After all the introductions had been made – using role titles in place of names, obviously – the prime minister's assistant led us in the direction of the city centre. I didn't want to be caught out searching for names again, so I'd come up with the idea of naming people in alphabetical order. As such, the assistant was Apple. It didn't matter what I called her, so long as I was consistent. Her translator would convert it into her name for herself. Other people's devices would use their name for her.

'So, Apple,' I said as we walked. 'How do people feel about the evacuation? Is everyone ready to go?'

Apple's four lower legs were covered in fur and ended in fuzzy little paws. Her torso was vaguely humanoid, but also covered in fur. Her ears and facial features were sort of feline.

She turned her head towards me for the first time, her expression unreadable. 'Many people don' believe there's ought wrong.' For no reason that I could discern, Holly had given her the voice and accent of a bored Yorkshire teen.

'How is that even possible? Hasn't it been months since it was first discovered?' Rincy tripped over a root lurking in the orange grass.

Apple purred – a low, rumbly sound. 'Years, actually.'

Bexley hoisted Rincy back to her feet. 'But then surely it

makes even less sense for people to deny reality, doesn't it? Like, how can people pretend there's nothing wrong?'

Apple stepped daintily over a flower bed – well, a bubble bed. She carried on walking without a glance back at us. 'Come on. Keep up.'

At the edge of the park, a car waited. Apple climbed gracefully in. The rest of us followed – but with less grace. Still not looking up from her phone, Apple pulled the door closed. As the vehicle moved away from the kerb, she licked her paw and groomed herself while staring at her own image on screen.

The conversation seemed to be over. A few minutes later, we pulled up outside a lemon yellow prefab building. The four of us approached. Instead of an ordinary door, it had ... well ... a giant cat flap. A round entryway dilated open about half a metre above the ground. I was tall enough to step over it, but Bexley had to take it at a run in order to leap over the threshold. Apple and Rincy both climbed over it easily – though the former did so with significantly more agility than the latter. Rincy sort of belly flopped through.

Apple sauntered down a short hallway, still tapping away on her phone.

I looked at Bexley and Rincy. 'Are we meant to follow?'

Bexley shrugged and set out after her.

'Spock is requesting to speak with you,' said Holly as I followed Bexley and Apple down the hall. 'Shall I put her through or decline the call?' Spock had an unfortunate tendency to call me every few minutes whenever we were separated.

'Can you tell her I'll call her back as soon as I can, please?'

'Done.'

Apple cranked the handle to open another cat flap/portal.

She didn't enter the room herself but held one arm up as if to indicate we should enter.

The office was small, so I helped Bexley clamber over rather than watch her take another flying leap – which would probably end in her crashing into the room's occupant, a stripy purplish-grey cat-person. Continuing my alphabetic theme, I dubbed this person Bob.

'Good morning, good morning. As you know,' Bob said, 'I'm the prime minister of Dave.' For the record, we did not – at that point – know any such thing. 'I'm very pleased we've been able to provide you this opportunity. It's a great honour.'

A great honour for whom … I wasn't sure.

'I'll get right to the point.' She pushed a glass of water off her sleek, glamorous desk. 'As you know, my people some-times find it … difficult to accept harsh truths. Comfortable alternative facts are often easier to accept in the face of so much loss.'

Instinctively, I bent down and picked up the glass from the floor. It had a lid, so the contents were still intact. I made to set it back on the desk, then thought better of it and set it on the floor next to the weird stool I was sitting on.

Bob twisted around and lifted one of her feet to scratch her ear. 'Moreover, until eight months ago, the government was led by an astronomy sceptic. The former prime minister mocked the scientists. As you know, she called their forecasts "judgements of ruin" and portrayed the researchers and aca-demics as "doomsayers". Most people on Dave thought the theories were fantastic fables designed to undermine the government. Many continue to believe that.'

Her story was all too familiar to me, so I said nothing. Rincy pulled items out of her bag and shuffled them on her lap.

'Hang on,' Bexley said. 'But surely you can tell people that science is real and that, you know, the threat is imminent. Like, you've literally got days to get everyone off this planet. Days. You know?'

Bob tapped a few keys on her keyboard. 'As you know, the proponents of astronomy scepticism now say that the science purists were successful in their efforts to subvert the government. They believe that malevolent forces interfered in order to overthrow the rightful leader.'

Rincy looked up from her pile of stuff. 'No one really thinks that, though, do they? I mean, the science on this is absolutely clear. You have to get everyone off this planet in the next three and a half *days*.'

'Yes, obviously,' Bob said, 'it's imperative you evacuate my people expediently. *My people* will be safely away from planet Dave in under three days. I have the Galactic Council's word on this.' Something about the way she said it rubbed me the wrong way – though I couldn't say why. She looked directly at Rincy. 'So, what's your plan? How will you make it happen?'

Rincy picked up her tablet, removed something that was stuck to the screen, and started clicking buttons.

Part of me worried she was going to subject us all to another embarrassing display of her personal entertainment files or give us another demonstration of her plan that wasn't a plan. But instead she simply said, 'I've arranged for vehicles that can carry groups of up to seventy-two people to a waiting cargo ship that will serve as a transfer station.'

I leant forwards in my seat. 'What we need from you, Bob, is details of your end of the arrangements.'

Bob stopped grooming herself long enough to glare at me. 'My end of...' She glided into the space between me and her desk. Arching her back, she rubbed herself along the edge of her desk and hissed. 'As you know, we hired you to enact the evacuation. *You* are making the arrangements for us. I can't believe you'd want to leave us here to die.'

'No one said anything about leaving you,' said Rincy. 'I'm sure Lem didn't mean that – did you, Lem?'

I leant away from Bob. The allergy medicine BB made was powerful enough to let me exist in a room with Bexley, but having a giant cat basically straddle me at the same time might be pushing it a bit too far. 'What? No, of course not,' I spluttered. 'I just meant we need to understand how people will be organised. How will they know when it's their turn to leave? Or which queue to join? How much stuff will each person be allowed? Are there any pets?'

Rincy flapped her little arms at me. 'All right, all right. I think we get your point. But you can't seriously expect the prime minister to look after these trivialities herself.'

'Of course, I'm sorry, Bob.' My eyebrow twitched as I pressed my fingers to my temple. 'Is there someone else here who can help co-ordinate things from your end? Maybe Apple?'

Bob stopped rubbing herself on Rincy's chair and took a literal swipe at me. She didn't actually make contact – but she hissed again and showed me her claws. 'Apple works for me. She doesn't have capacity to do your job as well.'

Bexley moved to put herself between Bob and me. 'We're talking about people's lives. Four thousand people. I mean, I'm sure you are super-duper important and I get that Apple's job probably keeps her busy all day, every day – but your lives are at stake. If we don't get everyone off this planet...'

Bexley looked around. 'Hey, you haven't packed. Shouldn't you basically be ready to go by now? I mean, the last time I had to move, I left everything to the last minute and it made everything so much harder than it needed to be –

and that was only one house. My dads are always reminding me to be organised but I never learn. Anyways, what I'm trying to say is, you need to leave, like, today.'

Bob licked her paw and rubbed her face. 'My people are paying good money for this evacuation. The arrangements are your concern, not mine.'

I bit back an angry retort. It wouldn't solve anything to lose my temper. Back on Earth I'd worked as an IT project manager in financial services – I'd dealt with plenty of self-important clients. Every front-office dude-bro I'd ever met thought I should be able to meet his team's needs without anyone actually telling me what those needs were.

'We've got four thousand people to evacuate and only two getoffs,' I said. Ground-to-orbit vehicles was too much of a mouthful, so I'd tried abbreviating that to GTOVs – and that pretty quickly morphed into getoffs. 'Each getoff can carry up to seventy-two people at a time. Allowing for loading and unloading, the round trip is probably no less than an hour. Even if we operate non-stop from the moment the *Egg* arrives, and we take people only, no goods beyond what people are carrying, it's still going to take twenty-eight solid hours to get everyone.'

I was surprised – shocked, really – to find that the basics hadn't been handled in advance of our arrival. 'We need to know who's responsible for the logistics.'

Bob stopped licking her paw and stared at me. 'What do you mean "Who is responsible for the logistics?" What do you think you're doing here? Is this a sightseeing trip to you? Are we animals in a zoo you're here to gawp at? You are here to work. How you get that work done is not my concern. The only thing I care about is that you accomplish your task.'

I resisted the urge to pinch the bridge of my nose. They

might not recognise the body language but still... 'But how will—'

Rincy pulled herself up to her full height. 'All right, Lem. I think we get the picture. The PM is a very busy person.'

'It's true. I am,' said Bob. 'Still, I suppose I can loan you Apple for an hour to answer your questions. As far as communicating with the public... As you know, we've arranged a press conference. You can make a statement to the journalists and they will ask you questions.' She turned her back on us and walked towards the window behind her desk. 'Now get out. I have work to do.'

5 / DISASTER-PLATYPUS

Leaving Bob to get on with her important prime minister things, we went straight into a meeting with Apple. We worked out an agreement whereby each individual could bring twenty kilograms of stuff – roughly the same amount as luggage allowance you get on an international flight.

Although Bexley was making a holo-record of the meeting, I made notes on my phone as quickly as I could. The act of taking notes helped me remember details. 'And what about pets?' I struggled to keep my eyes from falling shut.

There was a pause that suggested the word wasn't quite translating.

'Oh aye,' Apple said, while admiring her own reflection on her phone screen. She'd been on that thing the entire time. I still couldn't tell if she was talking to anyone or recording herself or just looking at herself. She tapped and clicked the hour away. 'Tha mean t' kobolds, right? Aye, I think people should probably be allowed to bring their kobolds – if there's room.'

I raised my hands. 'I wasn't suggesting we leave them to

die. It's more that I'm trying to get a handle on how many trips the getoffs need to make.'

Rincy *finally* seemed to be getting the idea that maybe an actual plan wasn't such a terrible idea. 'The kobolds should come, of course, but I think any goods they require should count towards the person's allowance.' We all agreed to that and then Rincy excused herself to take a call in the hallway.

I entered the figures for the weight and size of the average kobold into my spreadsheet as well as Apple's best guess at how many there were. 'Right. If we're to have any hope of getting everyone safely off the planet, we need to get people moving within the next couple of hours.'

Rincy clambered back through the room's portal. 'That was the captain of the *Egg*. They've just arrived and we've got seven other ships now as well. The rest should all be arriving over the next six hours or so. I've asked the captain to bring the getoffs down so we can get things started.'

The plan was to call people based on postcode. We'd work it like airplane boarding calls: rows eighteen through twenty-one followed by rows fourteen through twenty-one. That kind of thing.

The press conference was a whirlwind affair – except with a room full of cats who didn't actually seem that interested in anything we had to say. Maybe all press conferences were like that. I'd seen the odd one on telly, but I'd never been part of one before.

Rincy read a statement advising people to head to the evac site when it was their turn. She told people how much they could bring and how it should be packed – everything in the speech we'd all agreed. But then there was a barrage of questions – and I was punched in the gut by how much people were missing the point.

Even though Rincy made it abundantly clear that there

was just over three days until impact, the locals didn't seem to have any sense of urgency.

A duck egg blue plenti was the first to speak. 'Why haven't you organised by clan instead? Do you not think the families that have been around longest should have more rights?'

'How can you expect people to pack up their whole lives in just a few hours?' asked a peach tabby.

'Why weren't we given more notice?'

'Why must this evacuation be this week? The town fair is next month and surely you agree it would be more convenient to go after that.'

'Will there be organic meals on the ships?'

Rincy may be a disaster-platypus ninety per cent of the time, but to my immense surprise she held it together. I don't know how she did it. I reconsidered my estimate of her. Clearly, she wasn't entirely without skill – just not in the field of project management.

It was too much. If I'd been speaking, I'd have turned and walked off the platform. But she made a passionate, coherent, barnstormer of a speech, conveying the urgency of the situation. Then she repeated the message of where people should go and urged everyone to take this seriously.

I hoped it was enough.

———

We returned to our ships to take a few hours of rest. Even though it was barely lunchtime in Catford, it was nearly midnight on the *Teapot*. Rincy joined us for a quick working dinner as we discussed the next stage of the plans. BB had already gone to bed when we sat down in the mess, but the rest of the *Teapot*'s crew gathered. As before, Spock tried desperately to get close to Rincy – constantly sniffing and licking her.

Rincy declined any food, but Aurora made dinner for the rest of us while we talked. She blended the nutrient porridge to provide optimal nutrition for each of us. And she tailored it to our flavour preferences too. Bexley tended to go for things that smelled like a lot of grass or hay. Well, to me they did. She assured me I was missing out on a world of different flavours.

Spock, predictable as she was, chose sweet potato vindaloo.

'You know what,' I said when Aurora asked me for my preference. 'I'm going to have the vindaloo too, please. It's perfect. Would you mind doing me a lager to go along with it?' It wouldn't actually be beer – but it would smell and taste like it.

Aurora's normal glittery rainbow glowed slightly more royal blue than usual. 'But prepare that one separate from your food, yes?' Her voice was buttery soft in my ear.

I nodded. 'Are you sure you don't mind? I don't like to think of you being stuck in the kitchen or scrubbing the toilets all the time.'

'All work has value and I enjoy what I do.' Aurora extended a nebulous appendage and ran it through my hair, tickling me.

———

The moment Spock finished eating, she was back fawning over Rincy. I swatted her away when she got to be too much.

Spock glared at me. 'Rude.'

'We'll take it in turns,' Rincy said, 'to oversee the loading of the pods. The kobolds are about the size of plentitudian children, so each getoff can fit seventy-two people or pets. Babies or very small pets may travel with a parent or guardian, but most will require their own seat.'

'We need—' My words were cut off by a sneak-attack yawn. 'Sorry. I know we have to get back down there and start moving people. But I'm dead on my feet here. I need at least a few hours of sleep.'

Bexley patted my knee. 'You're okay, sweetie. You go get some rest. We'll be all right. Rincy, Henry, how about the three of us take the first shift?'

I promised to join them after I'd caught a bit of kip. Aurora agreed to join us when BB was up. Much to her chagrin, Spock would stay on the *Teapot*.

Rincy patted Spock's face as she stood up. 'We've all got our work cut out for us. Lem, you seem to have a flair for this sort of work. When I'm not available, you're in charge on site. I'd like you to be my second in command for this operation – if that's okay with you?'

In spite of my exhaustion – or possibly exacerbated by it – I felt a genuine thrill at her request. 'Sure, er… Yeah, that's absolutely fine. Happy to help.' Ever since Spock and I decided to stay on the *Teapot*, I'd been bristling at how useless I felt so much of the time.

Although I always tried to contribute my fair share of effort to every job we took, there didn't seem to be much call for a project manager in space. Which meant that I spent a lot of time feeling like a third wheel – or else struggling to complete tasks that were so far outside my comfort zone, I'd need a history book just to remind me I'd ever been good at anything. So, yeah, it was nice to be recognised.

I stood up. 'I'll see you lot in a bit. I'll set my alarm for four and join you as soon as I can get down there.'

Bexley got off the sofa as well. 'Right. We've got a population to evacuate. I've never been part of a mission like this one. Then again, I'm not sure there's ever been a mission quite like it. Like, there was one I read about in school. Well, whatever, I should let you get to bed. I'll tell you about it some other time.'

————

A little over three hours later, Holly startled me into waking up. Normally, it *told* me to wake up. Normal pitch and volume. But a while back I'd come up with an idea for when I needed extra help: I asked it to sing pop songs to me. Not *play* them; *sing* them. In its own voice.

Holly sang Britney Spears's 'Toxic' at me at full blast. Like, it would've woken the entire ship if these walls weren't solid … whatever the hell they were.

As it was, Spock fell out of bed and glared at me. 'Rude.'

'I'm not going to get much sleep this week, am I?'

'Adult humans are advised to get eight hours of sleep per night,' said Holly unhelpfully. 'Based on the schedule for this mission, it's likely you'll get half that amount over the next few days.'

'Shut up, Holly.' I didn't need it telling me what I already knew. 'That was a rhetorical question.'

To its credit, Holly shut up.

I plodded into the bathroom and did what I went to do. A few minutes later, Spock and I trudged our way down to the kitchen. Well, I trudged; she padded.

Aurora greeted us warmly.

Spock was her usual self. 'Hello, friend. Feed Spock?'

'In a minute, dear. Lem, I figured you'd be in a rush, so I got some of those meal bars ready for you. But I assumed you'd want to make your own beverage.' Aurora refused to make anything caffeinated for me. She could make water smell and taste like the finest latte known to humankind. But if I wanted anything with caffeine, I was on my own.

'Cheers, Aurora.' I shoved the bars in my pocket and opened the cupboard where I'd stashed my not-so-secret supply.

On one of the planets we'd visited before we'd picked up the trelane, I'd discovered a mild stimulant. BB wasn't happy about it, but she admitted it wasn't much worse than coffee.

I scooped some of the orange powder into my travel mug and then filled it with hot water. When the powder and water made contact, they kicked off a chemical reaction. It released a floral fragrance and turned the liquid bright purple. The resulting concoction tasted faintly of Marmite. Only sweeter. And it was caffeinated to the high heavens – exactly what I needed this morning.

I'd started off calling it heliotrocha, a portmanteau of heliotrope and mocha – but lately this had morphed into helbru. I took a sip and sighed deeply. Then I screwed the lid on tight – I planned on drinking it, not wearing it.

'I heard from Henry a little while ago,' said Aurora. 'She's keen for you to head down as soon as you're ready to go.'

I nodded. 'Did she say how it was going?'

We exited the kitchen, turning left towards the transporter room.

'Well,' she drew the word out for several beats. 'In our brief conversation, she called Bob a parking brake, denounced the entire species, declared it would be a mercy to let them die, and said it would be easier to persuade a group of pandas to attend an orgy.'

My oxygen mini-mask waited on a counter in the transporter room. Once I'd put it on, I picked a pod and pulled open the door. I stroked Spock's head. 'You be a good girl.

Aurora will get you your breakfast as soon as I'm gone. I'll see you in a few hours.'

Her lip quivered. 'Spock not come? Spock alone?'

Letting the pod door fall closed, I knelt down in front of her. 'You'll be fine, sweetie. You stay here with Aurora. She'll make you breakfast and then you can take a nap. Later, Bexley will come and play ball with you, yeah?'

Spock stood up and danced in circles. 'Bexley? Where Bexley? No see.'

I chuckled. Why hadn't I learnt better than to make a series of statements? 'I'll see you soon. You be good.' But she was off in search of Bexley, who was still down on the planet. I turned to Aurora. 'You'll get her some breakfast as soon as I'm gone, yeah?'

'Of course,' Aurora said as I climbed into the pod and fastened my seatbelt. She stretched out an ethereal nub and ran it through my hair. 'Just as soon as you're away.'

'Thanks.' I pulled the pod door closed, locking myself into the coffin-like space. Apparently some newer models of pod had viewing screens on the inside – though I didn't know how anyone could pay attention to anything other than their own existential dread while travelling by transporter. I'd never jumped out of a plane – but I imagined this was a lot like parachuting. If you had to make the leap blindfolded, that is.

Usually, at the end of a transporter journey, I felt a sudden awareness that I was no longer moving. This time, the smooth but terrifying motion of the voyage was followed by a series of rapid, jerky motions. It felt like I was tumbling over Niagara Falls in a barrel. 'What's going on, Aurora?'

In my ear, Aurora's smooth, buttery tones made a counterpoint to my rising panic. 'Suggest you remain where you are for a few minutes, Lem. Protesters have driven a bus into one of the getoffs. I believe they sideswiped your pod as well. I'll let you know when it's safe to exit.'

'They what? Why would anyone— Never mind. I'll find out soon enough. Is everyone okay?'

'Nothing from anyone else yet,' she replied.

'Bexley is requesting to speak with you,' said Holly. 'Shall I put her through or decline the call?'

'Sync her into my call with Aurora, please, Holly.'

'Lem!' Bexley sounded breathless. 'Are you okay? I saw a pod coming down. I thought it might be you so I was running over towards it when it occurred to me, it might not be you and I might be running for no reason and wouldn't that be ridiculous? But anyways, then the protesters came out of nowhere. Well, not out of nowhere. I mean, there have been protesters here all day. But the ones in the bus ... well, I don't know. They haven't actually damaged the getoff, but some of them are hurt. Rincy sent someone to fetch some paramedics – and now she's rounding up the rest of the protesters. But is it you in there?'

I struggled to process all that. 'Yeah, it's me. But what the hell? Why would anyone protest a rescue mission?'

'Um.' Bexley paused. 'I don't think these ones were protesting the evacuation. Or rather, they're protesting the fact it didn't come sooner. Or maybe later. Or that people weren't taking the threat seriously. I'm not sure exactly. We've had other ones protesting the evacuation, though. And some protesting the kobolds. I think there was a group who were angry about ... I'm not sure, actually.'

'Huh,' was all I could think to reply as I sat ensconced in my gel-lined pod.

'Henry is requesting to speak with you,' said Holly. 'Shall I put her through or decline the call?'

'Sync her in as well, please, Holly,' I said. 'Henry? Are you okay?'

'No, you cockles,' unswore Henry. 'I'm stuck in a plucky rut. Someone's going to have to come pull me out.'

I swung my door open, only to discover I was leaning back at a forty-five-degree angle. 'You're what?' I scrambled up and out of the pod and jumped to the ground. 'Where are you?' I twirled around, struggling to get my bearings. It was the same pod park we'd set down in yesterday. But there was a new building in the middle of what had been open space. The building looked undamaged – but there was a strange turquoise vehicle mashed into the side of it. It appeared to have been abandoned as there wasn't anyone in it or even hanging around it.

Bexley galloped towards me and practically leapt into my arms. 'You're okay! I'm so glad you're all right.'

'Cheers,' I said. 'Likewise. But er... where's Henry? We should go find her. Do you know where she was before —'

'I'm still on the line, you pickle.' Henry guided us to where she was, just the other side of the building – which turned out to be the getoff. 'Not one word out of you, ankle parkas. Not one scabby word.'

Bexley's enormous jaw fell slack. 'Oh, Henry! What happened?'

Henry lay on her back next to an uprooted tree. Or her front, I suppose. She was a featureless cylinder – no real directionality to speak of. A signpost and branches of a tree pinned her in place. 'What do you mean, "What happened?" I fell in a cupping hole, didn't I?'

'Hang on, Henry,' I said as Bexley and I rushed to her aid. 'We'll get you out of there.'

Bexley hefted the signpost out of the ground and tossed it aside. 'I think if we just move these branches here...' She pulled a few grey branches and orange leaves aside. 'There, if I hold these like this ... can you pull Henry out, Lem?'

Henry extruded what looked like a handle. 'Here, grab this – and I swear if you tell a single goat-herding person about this I will make your life a barking nightmare. Forever.'

I bit my lip. 'I promise. And I'll try not to touch you any more than I absolutely have to.' Taking hold of the proffered handle, I put all my weight into my task. 'Oof! Why the hell do you weigh so much? Are you made of lead?'

Before Henry could reply, Bexley snapped off a branch and studied it. 'I'm sorry, tree. I don't mean to hurt you. Though, when I think of it, you're probably not going to last much longer anyways. But I need to pull my friend out.'

'The cuffing tree accepts your apology,' growled Henry. 'Now will you cheese curds hurry up and get me out of here?'

It took a few minutes, but Bexley managed to free Henry from the tree's embrace. And I burnt a week's worth of calories hauling her upright. For her part, Henry unswore a family friendly blue streak at us the whole time.

I bent over next to the tangled mess, bracing myself against my knees, breathing hard. Bexley stood up, shook herself off, and nickered.

Henry produced a little vacuum hose and cleaned herself off. 'We shall never speak of this again.' Retracting the vacuum, she extended a mirror on a stick and inspected herself. 'Thank you, though. But seriously, never mention it.'

I bit my lip to keep from – I wasn't sure whether I was trying not to let her see me smile or laugh or maybe scream. 'You're welcome, Henry.' I pulled my mug of helbru from my bag and unscrewed the lid. 'Now, how many pods got off overnight? Is everything on track?' I took a sip of the life-giving stimulant.

Bexley pushed her short mane over her shoulder – a futile move, as it swung back into her face. 'Yeah, about that… The good news is that a few people from the other ships came down to help. Rincy sent them into town to try to encourage more plenties to join us.'

I was missing something. 'That's great. So you had more support than expected.' I checked my watch. 'The fifth getoff should be lifting off now. Are we on track?'

Bexley looked away.

Henry rolled towards me on the purple concrete. 'One. Frolicking one, all right? Happy now? While you've been powered down, we've been herding cats. And let me tell you, I don't know what you *thought* was going to happen – but it turns out, these people do not want to leave.' She extended a hooked implement in my direction and whirled it around.

My shoulders fell. 'What?'

'Spock is requesting to speak with you,' said Holly. 'Shall I put her through or decline the call?'

'Not now, Holly. Tell her I'll call her back as soon as I'm free.' I shouldn't have snapped, but the timing was terrible. If anything was genuinely wrong, her device would send me an alert.

Bexley pushed her forelock down over her long face. 'Some people show up – but mostly not when it's actually their turn. We try to encourage them to board anyways, but they usually just tell us they're waiting for someone or they're checking things out or they're only there to lecture us on how astronomy is all a scam started by scientists and listen here, youngster, this colony has had quite enough of experts, thank you very much.' She blew out noisily, vibrating her big, horsey nostrils.

Bexley dropped down onto her haunches and, for the first time, I noticed the signs of sheer exhaustion. She didn't sleep much – maybe three hours a night and a one-hour nap in the day. To my mind, she generally seemed tireless. But in that moment, she looked like she was ready to crash right there on the purple tarmac.

I knelt down and put my hand on her shoulder. 'Do you have enough energy to join Henry in catching me up on where we're at? Then I'll take over for you so you can get some sleep.'

She tapped her hooves on the ground in front of her

softly. 'Sure, I can do that. Just give me a minute to catch my breath and take a drink.'

I turned to Henry. 'What about you? How are you feeling? Do you need to recharge?'

'I'm good, sandwich,' she replied. 'I've got enough battery for another six hours or so. You just focus on getting us back on track – if you can.'

I scanned the evac site and beyond, towards the centre of Catford. There were dozens of plenties walking around, hither and thither. Some of them pottered, others meandered, and a few appeared to be gambolling playfully. The remnants of at least one picnic was scattered across the orange grass beyond the edge of the pavement. Aside from the bus that crashed into the getoff, everything looked like a social event.

Bexley showed me how she was tracking people who checked in and where they should store their stuff.

With a melodramatic sigh, I put my hands on my hips. 'So, we're basically flight attendants – but for people who don't want to travel.'

Bexley narrowed her eyes. 'I'm not entirely certain I understood that reference ... but it sounds about right.'

'Okay,' I said. 'Anyway, you go get some sleep. Henry and I will see if we can get this mission back on target – or at least not let it slide further off. Come join us when you're ready.'

Bexley clambered to her feet and tapped her hooves in the air in front of herself. 'Thanks. I'll see you in a few hours.' She touched my elbow as she headed for the pod I'd just left.

Henry and I made for the entrance to the getoff. 'Have any members of the local government come by to assist?'

'Have they fork.'

Was that a Scotticism? 'Huh. Apple said she'd have a word

with Bob about sending us some help.' This was getting progressively worse.

'That pumpkin of a prime minister came by to tell us all how grateful we should be for the opportunity. She's a carping delight.'

I rolled my eyes. 'Of course she did.' That wasn't exactly surprising. We headed into the getoff so I could see how the loading was proceeding. 'Er, Henry?' I gawped at the empty interior of the vehicle.

Henry rolled up alongside me. 'Oh, it's finally dawned on you that we weren't cracking making it up, has it?'

I extended my arms and spun around. 'Where is everyone? What the hell is going on?' I demanded of no one in particular. Not one of the seventy-two seats was occupied. A handful had stuff on them and maybe a dozen storage lockers had been closed. Most were empty and open.

As we stood there, a couple of plenties walked through the door. 'Hi, welcome. Pick a seat, any seat. If you've got —'

Their tails swished slowly. One stepped towards me and bared her teeth. 'Oh, we're not staying. You can't fool us. We're part of the protest.' The pair stepped back out, leaving us alone again.

'Henry, what the actual —'

I spun around, startled by a noise behind me. 'Hi. Oh.' Standing in the doorway was a small blue bipedal lizard-ish creature carrying large duffle bags. 'Hi there. You must be one of the kobolds I've heard about. Welcome.'

The kobold made as wide a path around Henry and me as was possible in the confines of the vehicle.

'Oh, er, okay.' The kobold approached a locker and placed her bags into it. Then she turned around and left.

'Henry, what the hell is…?'

'Sooner or later,' said Henry, 'you're going to have to finish one of those questions, cheese curd.'

I shook my head to clear it. 'Where are the plenties? Where's all their stuff? If only one transport has gone, then this one's been sitting here for, what, four hours? Where is everyone?'

If Henry had shoulders, I got the distinct impression she would have shrugged them. 'Your guess – in this exceptionally rare instance – is as good as mine.'

I turned and headed back out the door. The sky was deeper – more teal than turquoise. Fat drops of lemon-scented rain fell on me.

Marching straight to the nearest group of plenties, I waved in greeting. 'Hi.' They were grouped in a circle, sitting on the orange grass.

They looked up at me, curiosity battling boredom in their expressions. Or was that all in my head? 'Hello,' said one of them.

I put my hands on my hips – then reminded myself I needed to be persuasive, not petulant. Lowering my hands to my sides, I said. 'Hi, welcome. There's ample room on this transport. You can go ahead and board now.'

One of the plenties scratched behind her ear with one of her feet. 'No thanks. We'll wait for a later one. There's no rush.'

Touching my fingers to my temples, I stammered, 'Th-there is, though. There is absolutely a rush. You understand the severity of what's happening, right? Your world is going to be uninhabitable.'

Her friend stood up, stretched to her full height, and looked me in the eye. 'Yes, actually, we do. We campaigned *for* the current government. I even created a petition, calling for action within the next two and a half years.' Beneath the translated words Holly spoke, I could hear the hissing and growling sounds of the plenti's actual speech.

Since I couldn't seem to unclench my fists, I hid them behind my back. 'You don't have two and a half years. You don't have two and a half weeks. This world will be destroyed in a few *days*. Please—' My voice cracked on the word. 'Please board. Come with me if you want to live.'

'Fine,' said the first one. She stood up and beckoned the group to join her. And then they headed away from where the getoff was parked.

'Hey,' I called out to the departing group. 'Where are you going? The getoff is right here.' I looked down at Henry, who had wheeled up beside me at some point.

One of them faced me while still walking away. 'We're going home to pack.'

I groaned. 'Okay, well come back as quick as you can. And bring all your friends and family.' To Henry, I added, 'We should see who else we can round up. Do you want to go that way?' I pointed in a random direction. 'And I'll go the other way. Ping me if you run into trouble or – I don't know – if any more trees fall on you.'

Henry rolled away. 'Har har. Such hilarity, sandwich. I can hardly keep my seams from bursting.'

As I made my way across the site, I heard a new voice.

'… think it might be worse than we've been told.'

A second voice replied, 'We have to warn the others. We can't leave them here to die.'

A third added, 'We don't have much choice in the matter, though, do we?'

As I got closer, I expected to see a group of plenties. Instead, I was confronted with three of the pets or service animals or whatever they were. Kobolds.

I didn't want to scare them, so I tried to be as calm and friendly as I could. 'Hi.'

The three kobolds shrieked and ran in different directions.

'Spock is requesting to speak with you,' said Holly. 'Shall I put her through or decline the call?'

'Seriously, Holly. Not now,' I said. 'I will call her back – I promise.'

I selected one of the kobolds at random and followed her. 'Hey, I won't hurt you! I want to help. Please let me help.' But it was too late. She'd disappeared from view. Glancing around, I couldn't see the others either.

'Holly, get Henry on the line. It's urgent.'

'What now?' Henry's posh, androgynous voice sounded in my ear. 'I thought you wanted me out here, persuading these frocking kitties to board the getoff.'

'Where are you, Henry? I'll come to you.'

In the distance, a flicker caught my eye – like a sort of clacks or semaphore. Flashing black and white. I made for that direction. 'Henry,' I shouted. 'The kobolds.'

Henry wheeled towards me. 'What about them?'

She stood near a group of plenties, so I motioned for her to come away a bit. 'They definitely told us they were pets, right? Animals. Like Spock. Not people.'

Henry prodded me with a fork. 'All this time and you still have the audacity to disrespect Spock. She's not your property.'

'Not now, Henry,' I snapped. 'You know what I mean.

The plenties told us the kobolds were their pets, right? I'm not making that up, am I?'

'I wasn't there, meatsack,' said Henry. 'But that's what both Rincy and Bexley told me. Besides, you're not imaginative enough to make that up.'

'Cheers,' I said in what I hoped was a witheringly sarcastic tone.

Henry turned in a circle. 'Rincy said the kobolds don't have speech – which makes them less sapient than Spock. And even less than you.'

I ignored the jibe. 'So, why did I just find a group of them carrying on an intelligent conversation?'

Henry poked me with some sort of blunt instrument. 'Are you sure you recognise intelligent speech?'

'Yes, thank you. I am one hundred per cent certain. They did *not* sound like sub-sapients.' I rubbed my temple as I tried to remember exactly what I'd heard. 'Take Spock for example. Holly translates her speech for me – but the ideas she conveys are animalistic in nature, focused on immediate needs and wants. What I heard from the kobolds was way more mature – focused outwardly and thinking about the future.'

'Tell me what they said,' Henry replied. 'As precisely as your bloated, meat-based CPU will allow.'

I repeated the brief snippet of what I'd overheard.

'Frolicking guacamole stake bollards,' unswore Henry. 'Bob – that scabby morphing rocker lied to us. Where are they now?'

I scratched my head. 'Who, Bob? I've no idea.'

'No, you pickle,' Henry said. 'Where are the kobolds? We need to talk to them.'

'Oh. They ran away as soon as they saw me.' I shook my head. 'And before you call me a great oaf or a panini or a bag of water or whatever, yes… I did try *not* to scare them. What should we do?'

'Well,' said Henry. 'I suppose the first thing is to let Rincy know.'

I glanced around – I hadn't seen her since returning to the planet. 'Shouldn't she be here?'

Henry made a noise that sounded like a bitter laugh. 'I got a message from her. She went with the injured protesters to the hospital and then from there to the prison to check on the ones that were arrested. She wants them held in custody on the *Egg*, not down here – so now she's arguing with the cops.'

I decided not to make the obvious custard pun aloud. Even if it translated, which it wouldn't, Henry would only deride my childish sense of humour. 'We do need to bring her up to speed.' I dropped my voice a bit. 'Hey, Holly? Can you message Rincy and ask her to join us at the evac site as soon as she can, please?'

'Sending now,' it replied.

'Does this discovery change anything, really?' Something was niggling at the back of my brain, but I couldn't quite grasp it.

'Think about it, meatsack,' said Henry. 'When we saw the kobold in the getoff earlier, what was she doing?'

'She put some bags in a storage locker.' I was still missing something.

Henry extruded a whisk and swished it around a bit. 'Whose bags?'

I was so close to figuring this out; I felt sure of it.

Bexley's bubbly voice distracted me. 'Hey, Lem, Henry. How's everything going? Have you had any more success in getting the plenties to board the getoffs?'

'The kobolds are sapient,' I blurted.

Bexley gripped me in a bear hug. Well, a horsey hug. Technically, a unicorn hug. 'Oh, oh my gosh. Wow. What?'

I repeated my story again.

'Oh, that's amazing,' Bexley said. 'Are they all from the same original planet? Because that would be so cool – two completely distinct species from... That's pretty much— Oh! Oh.' Both her hooves shot up to cover her mouth. 'Crap.'

I still couldn't put my finger on why this was a problem – and it left me feeling increasingly thick. 'What am I missing?'

Bexley gave me a pitying sort of look as Rincy arrived. 'Hi, all. I got your message, Lem. What's up?'

'The kobolds are sapient,' I said.

'Oh, that's interesting,' Rincy said. 'Except... Oh bollocks!' She raised her middle arm and rested her chin on her hand. 'Hang on, what happened? What made you reach this conclusion?'

As I repeated the story for the third time, even I was getting a bit tired of listening to me.

I was about to ask someone to tell me why this was such a big deal when Henry stabbed me in the leg with an appendage that looked like a tiny trowel. 'The kobold we saw earlier ... she put some bags in a locker, yes?'

I nodded.

Henry poked me with the little shovel again. 'Whose bags were they?'

'Hers.' I looked at my three friends. 'Weren't they? Wait – no. The kobolds don't have baggage allowance.'

Bexley put an arm around me. 'The plenties made themselves out as the kobolds' guardians. They told us their relationship to the kobolds was akin to a parent to a child or your relationship to Spock. You're responsible for Spock. You tell her what to do and where to go. Because she's an *immature* sapient. You wouldn't do those things if she were a *mature* sapient.'

I recalled thinking they must be like service animals or workhorses. Stealing a glance at Bexley, I cringed at my own internal use of the word workhorse. And it finally clicked in my brain. 'You can't —' My hand shot up to my face. 'They're *slaves*?'

Bexley tapped her hooves in the air and Henry wheeled in a circle.

'If they are sapient, as you surmise,' said Rincy. 'Then at the very least they're being oppressed.'

'How do we find them?' I asked. 'We need to talk to the kobolds. They shouldn't have to go with the plenties. I mean, obviously, we evacuate them as planned – but they shouldn't be made to go to the same destination as the plenties.'

Rincy waddled on the spot. 'Exactly.'

Bexley shifted her weight from foot to foot. 'Okay, what should we do now?'

I took a deep breath to give myself time to think. This was a lot – too much, honestly – but if we broke it down, it was a project, right? And I was a project manager. *Remove the emotion and think of it as a job*, I told myself. *This is just scope creep – you deal with scope creep all the time. Break it into pieces. What needs doing?*

I steepled my fingers beneath my chin as I tried to alter the plan on the fly. 'Okay, I think the most important thing is to speak to a representative of the kobolds.'

Rincy waved her hands. 'Good, thanks. I'm in so far over my head. I think we also need to confer with the minister back on Trantor.'

'It's against GU law to keep sapient beings as slaves, right?' I was pretty sure it was but I wanted confirmation again.

Bexley tapped her hooves in the air. 'It is, definitely. If the kobolds are sapient, the government will need to provide a separate haven for them. If they're even suspected to be sapient, then they're obligated to intervene.'

Rincy rolled her head side to side. 'True, true.'

'They seem pretty reluctant to speak to us, though,' said Bexley.

I blinked. 'I don't think we've got much choice – we have to talk to the local government. We should ask them what they know.'

'Parking pickles!' Henry revved her internal motor. 'I know, I know. We do need to confront them on this – but it needs to be separate from the conversation with the kobolds. We can't ask the slavers if we can speak to the enslaved. They'll want to participate in our conversation – or try to prevent us from speaking to the kobolds at all.'

'Good point,' I said. 'Okay, how about if Bexley and I go to Bob's office to find out what she knows?'

Rincy stroked her bill. 'Henry, perhaps you and I can try to convince some of the kobolds to speak to us?'

Bexley did a little hop on the spot. 'Oh, what about the getoff? Someone should stay here. You know, in case anyone shows up.'

'I agree,' said Rincy. 'Thank you – all of you. Even before this latest discovery, I was feeling overwhelmed. My expertise is media relations, not project management. I was on leave from my job with the GU, visiting my batchmate. I got this gig because I was passing through the sector on my way back. I'll ask the teams from the other ships to return to the evac site to oversee things here.'

Bexley put a hoof on Rincy's shoulder. 'It's okay. We're all in this together.'

It explained a lot. I felt for Rincy. I nodded at her, then at Henry. 'We'll see you in a bit. Good luck.'

Bexley and I headed into town. 'Er… I don't suppose you remember the way to Bob's office, do you?' The one time I'd been before, we'd been driven.

'Yeah, no, sorry,' replied Bexley – which was about as Toronto of a response as you could get. Holly had drawn Bexley's voice and accent from a Canadian colleague of mine back on Earth. Hence … Canadianisms. The translator worked figuratively, so rather than trying to explain one culture's euphemisms, colloquialisms, and idioms to someone from another, it used whatever closest approximation the listener would understand.

I stopped to survey the pretty town from the edge of the park. The buildings were low – no more than one or two storeys – and brightly coloured. The rain had stopped, leaving a rainbow in its wake. 'Hey, Holly?'

'Yes, Lem,' came its disembodied voice.

'Can you guide us to Bob's office from here, please?'

'Of course,' said Holly. 'If you walk, it will take approximately eleven minutes. Is that what you'd like to do?'

Following Holly's directions, we were soon at the civic centre. By local time, it was nearing the end of the workday. Another group of protesters milled about in front of the entrance – but I didn't catch what it was they were protesting. With no one to lead us, we had to ask at the front desk.

A pink-hued feline receptionist studied us. 'The prime minister is very busy. If you tell me why you need to see her, I may be able to arrange a meeting with one of her staff a few weeks from now.'

'A few weeks from now,' I spluttered. 'She *won't be here* a few weeks from now. By then, you'll all be sipping piña coladas on a space station somewhere safe. Maybe dreaming about what life will be like —'

The receptionist's claws peeked out from her fuchsia paws.

Bexley smoothed her mane with one hoof. 'What we're trying to say is that we're part of the team sent by the GU to evacuate planet Dave. We need to see Bob on urgent business relating to the withdrawal process.'

The claws retracted again. 'Fine. I'll send a message to Apple, Bob's assistant. She can decide whether to interrupt the prime minister.'

'Thank you,' I said. Bexley and I wandered over to a waiting area near the desk.

'Spock is requesting to speak with you,' said Holly. 'Shall I put her through or decline the call?'

As we waited for Bob to see us, I figured I may as well. 'Sure, Holly.' I pulled my phone out while the call connected. 'Hi, sweetie. What's up?'

Spock was sitting on the floor in Ten Backwards. The planet Dave loomed large in the window behind her. 'Where Lem go?'

I couldn't help but smile. 'I'm on the planet, remember? I have to help evacuate the plenties before their planet explodes.'

'Tasty kitties?' Drool formed at the edges of her mouth.

'Yes, Spock,' I said. 'That's them.'

'Bring tasty kitties?'

'Yes, Spock. We'll bring them.' A horrifying thought occurred to me. 'I mean, we're bringing them to save their lives. We're not bringing them for you to eat.'

'No eat tasty kitties?'

'No, Spock,' I said. 'No eat anyone. Look, I have to go

now. But I'll see you soon. I love you.' But she'd already disconnected.

After a few minutes, Apple stepped out from the area where the offices were, her eyes still glued to her phone. 'Come wi' me.'

Bexley and I followed her down the hall to a different room from the ones we'd used yesterday. Or this morning, I guess, depending on your perspective. Yesterday for me; but it had only been this morning for Apple.

I helped Bexley through the portal-door then climbed through myself. As I took my seat I said, 'Bob will be joining us, yes?'

Apple licked her paw and smoothed the fur on her cheeks – all without looking up from her phone. 'T' gaffer's busy.'

Bexley leaned forwards in her chair. 'Oh, I think she's going to want—'

I put a hand on Bexley's elbow. 'Apple, yesterday you told us the kobolds were pets.'

Apple tilted her head – eyes still on her screen. 'Aye. They're service animals. We care for them and feed them and they do tasks for us. I've got one. Been wi' me since I were a kitten.'

Bexley ground her teeth.

I pressed on. 'They are animals, though, right? Not mature sapients? I'm sure you said they don't speak.'

Apple's tail flicked out and wrapped around the handle that contracted the portal-door. 'Why?'

I shifted in my seat and crossed my legs. 'Earlier today, I overheard a conversation between several kobolds. You told us they lacked the power of speech.'

Instead of replying, Apple cranked the door handle open and climbed over the portal and out of the room.

Bexley and I looked at one another, both holding our breath for a moment.

'What just happened?'

Before Bexley could respond to my question, the door dilated again. Bob barged into the room, chest puffed out. She strutted to the chair next to mine and straddled it. Apple dropped into the one remaining chair, her nose still buried in her phone.

Bob extended a paw, a single terrifyingly long claw extended. She ran it down the side of my face. Her touch was gentle, but the implied threat was as clear as a flashing neon sign. 'So. I understand you believe you've made a discovery. Why don't you tell me what you *think* you witnessed?'

I'd worked in financial services long enough – I had a thick skin. In my career, I'd faced off to plenty of front-office bullies. Big swinging dicks they'd been called – which always seemed a horrifically transphobic phrase. And possibly misogynistic.

I smiled at Bob, flashing my teeth. 'Good morning, Prime Minister. Thank you for joining us. It's good of you to make time for us.' I took a calming breath. 'Today I overheard a conversation between a group of kobolds. An intelligent conversation.'

Bob extended her claws and scratched them along a rough stripe in the centre of the table. 'You heard them speaking, did you? What were they saying? Please ... tell me precisely what you *heard*.' The focus she put on the final word struck me as odd, though I couldn't put my finger on why.

I poured every ounce of professional friendliness I possessed into my expression. 'They were discussing the planetary crisis. One of them said it was worse than they'd been led to believe. A second one voiced similar concerns. She wanted to warn "the others".'

Bob returned my smile – in a way that made me shiver despite the room's warmth. 'I see. And of course you challenged them on this? Queried which others they meant? Asked clarifying questions, yes?'

Bexley leaned forwards in her chair and snorted.

'They ran away,' I said. 'I told them they had nothing to fear, but for some reason the kobolds are scared to come near us.'

'As you know,' Bob said, 'we've been very honest with you from the beginning that the kobolds possess ... a kind of low-level intelligence.' She hadn't, of course, told us any such thing. 'They have intellectual abilities equivalent to those of a small kitten. And some kobolds have been known to mimic certain words or phrases. What they lack, however, is the capacity for rational thought. And they cannot *speak*.'

Bob leaned down and licked her belly. 'The kobolds have been the subject of numerous research studies.' She chuckled – a deep sound that made bile rise in my throat. 'However, for you to arrive at the conclusion that it was an indication they were equal to our own intelligence ... well, I'm afraid it doesn't say much for your own reasoning.'

She stood up and – without another word – left the room. Apple spared us a single glance before following her boss.

Bexley and I looked at one another. 'I'm actually speechless,' she said. 'Me. I am without words. I don't think I've been speechless since I was a foal. You know me, I can talk the hind legs off a donkey. I could talk for my planet in the Olympics. Most of the time you can't get me to shut up. For me to be lost for words is basically –'

'I get it.' I nodded. 'But come on, we've still got work to do. Let's head back to the evac site.'

Bexley leaned in close. 'You don't believe her, do you?

Like, I think I know you well enough to trust that you can distinguish between mimicry and actual conversation.'

I put my hand on the portal-door crank handle. 'Like hell do I believe her. The kobolds I heard weren't mimicking anyone – they were talking. And they were scared. But we should stay quiet until we're away from this building. I don't want to be overheard.'

I spun the handle to dilate the door, then helped Bexley climb through. As we exited the building, we said goodbye to the hostile receptionist.

On the way back to the evac site, I finally said, 'What the hell was that all about? They really think we're ignorant, don't they? Did they think I couldn't tell the difference between speech and pure repetition?'

Bexley sneered. 'I know, right? They were so rude. Like, they think they can stop us from talking to the kobolds. And did you see the way Bob walked in there? She knew … I mean, she knew, right?'

I put my hand in Bexley's hoof. 'We can't be a party to their continued subjugation of a sapient species. But how do we stop it?' My stomach turned. We couldn't.

Bexley snorted. 'Right there with you, bud. We've got to find a way to help. I mean, we've got to get these people off this planet. Which means we have to talk to the government minister overseeing all this. She'll know what to do, right? Like, that's her job, no?'

I looked at the beautiful world around me. It was all so normal and yet so alien. 'It's so weird to think that everything here is going to be destroyed in three days. Weird? No, that's the wrong word. Scary?'

Bexley leaned in close and whispered. 'And now we have to find a way to evacuate a whole 'nother species and keep them safe from the plenties. Like, it's just too much, you know?'

'And we still don't know how to get in touch with any of the kobolds.' I stopped walking and looked at her. 'Bexley, what are we going to do?'

Her nostrils flared. 'Let's get back to the evac site and talk to the others.'

The second pod had returned from the *Egg*, filling up much of the available space.

Rincy hadn't had any luck tracking down kobolds who would speak to us. Henry had gone back up to the *Teapot* to recharge when BB and Aurora transported down. I didn't like to think of Spock being alone in a spaceship even for a few minutes, so I switched on the Spock-cam. It activated based on where she was – so it showed me an image of her sound asleep on the sofa in Ten Backwards. She was curled up with her brain clutched in her paws. I decided not to wake her.

When I told Rincy how Bob had reacted, she jabbed two hands into her sides. 'I'm going to march right down to her office and confront her.'

Aurora floated over to join us. 'Would you like me to join you, my dear?'

Rincy heaved out a sigh. 'I'd be grateful for your company. And your support.'

BB stepped forwards. 'The rest of us can stay here to load the pods.'

Rincy and Aurora had just left when Holly announced in its flat, mechanical voice, 'I have an incoming message for you, Lem. Unknown source. It says, "Café on the Park. Twenty minutes." Would you like me to provide directions?'

'Hang on.' I turned to the others. 'Did you get the same message?'

Bexley tapped her hooves in the air twice. 'The one about the café? Yeah.'

BB clucked. 'What's this? What message?'

Huh. 'Bexley and I were just invited to speak to a mysterious informant.'

Bexley looked up at me. 'We should go, right? Do you think we should go? Who could it be from? I don't think it's a trick, but I suppose it could be a trick.'

I smiled. The same thoughts had occurred to me. 'I don't know – but we'd better find out.'

'You go,' said BB. 'I'll call some of the people from the other ships to come and give me a hand. We'll all gather back here in a bit.'

———

The café Holly directed us to was outside, next to a teal building. At least we didn't have to climb through any giant cat flaps half a metre off the ground. A bar surrounded the purplish-grey trunk of a large tree. A dozen or so pretty tables surrounded the bar, under the orange canopy of leaves. The whole thing was dappled with warm sunlight filtered through a rainbow of leaves and bubble-flowers – a lovely place for a rest stop. Well, if you ignored the part about the forthcoming apocalypse, obviously.

'No one seems to be in any rush to leave this planet,' said Bexley. 'I don't get it. Like, have they forgotten a massive asteroid is going to hit in three days?' We placed our orders at the bar: a peppergrass smoothie for Bexley and a berry juice for me. We dropped leaflets on every table, urging people to get to the evac site as soon as they could. About half the tables were vacant, so we picked one at random.

Bexley took a dainty sip of her gold drink. 'Who do you think we're waiting for?'

I tried to get comfortable in a seat designed for a six-limbed cat-centaur. 'It's got to be either Apple or Bob, right? No one else knows.'

Bexley tapped her hoof on the edge of the table softly. 'My money's on Apple. Bob made her feelings pretty clear, don't you think?' Her nostrils flared briefly as she sniffed the air. 'Hey, isn't that the receptionist from the civic office?'

With my head facing Bexley, I swivelled my eyes as far as I could. There was definitely a pink plenti at the bar. 'I can't tell.'

With all the subtlety of Spock begging for breakfast, Bexley looked around, studying the various customers. 'Do you think she's our mysterious contact?' Bexley had many great qualities – subtlety wasn't one of them.

I kept my voice low. 'We'll find out soon, I guess.'

The bright pink cat paid for her drink and headed our way without looking at us. I dubbed her Charlie Jane – no, CJ.

Bexley opened her mouth to speak to her, but CJ flashed her claws in a sort of flicking motion. I took that as an indication she didn't want to be seen speaking to us.

CJ sat down at the table next to ours, keeping her back to us. For a few moments, nothing happened. But then, she said, 'I know why you were in the civic centre today. Such matters are highly controversial. But you are not alone in the conclusion you have drawn.'

'I knew it – I knew we were right about this,' Bexley whisper-squealed. CJ responded with a snappy flick of her tail.

'Discreet,' I whispered. Then, to CJ I added, 'We need to speak to the kobolds. Do they have a representative? Is there someone who'll talk to us? Can you facilitate that?'

'I would lose my job if even a tenuous connection to the kobold liberation movement were discovered.' The next few seconds passed in tense silence. At length, CJ said, 'There is someone. I can't promise she'll agree to meet with you. But I'll pass on a message – and I'll get her a translator device. She may not want to talk to you. But it's the best I can do, I'm afraid. I will not force her to listen to me. She may not even accept the translator – it's illegal for her to possess one.'

Out of the corner of my eye, I spied CJ stand up to leave. 'Wait,' I cried as quietly as I could. I tried to convey urgency without speaking loudly enough to draw attention to us. 'Please, there's so much more we need to ask you. Things we need to know.' But she was gone.

Bexley leaned back in her seat. 'What the —' She cut her own words off and whispered, 'Let's head back.'

———

Rincy and Aurora weren't back yet when we got to the site. People were finally beginning to trickle in. BB and the teams from the other ships had managed to load two more pods and get them off to the *Egg*. We were so far behind schedule. That asteroid was almost here.

One of the getoffs had landed and a crowd had gathered around.

BB lifted her wings in greeting as she headed over to join us.

'Looks like people are finally taking an interest,' I said.

She stretched a long vividly coloured wing in the direction of the getoff. 'Them?' She made a strange squawking sound. 'Alas, you're correct that they're taking an interest. But that's as far as it goes. They're not boarding – merely looking around. We and our getoffs are a curiosity to them – nothing more.'

I pinched the bridge of my nose. 'We need to launch this getoff in the next hour.' I raised my voice and called out for everyone to board.

A few of the plenties looked at me – but they all carried on milling about. A few wandered off.

As a group of plenties – all with spotted blue-grey fur – walked past, I heard one say, 'I don't know why they're acting like it's some big rush. Seems very rude to me.'

They carried on walking away as I shouted, 'There is a rush, actually. Dave is going to be hit by a planet-killing asteroid in three days.'

An amber tabby plenti looked me up and down. 'It's not like we're astronomy-denialists – if that's what you're insinuating. We're not.'

Bexley stepped in front of me. 'If people delay, we'll never get everyone off the planet in time. That asteroid won't wait.'

The crowd was dispersing. I chased after a group at random. It was time to crack out the maths. 'We have almost four thousand people to evacuate,' I called to everyone and no one. 'Each getoff can carry seventy-two people. Even with both getoffs working flat out, making a round trip every hour and a half, it will take us more than two days to complete the evacuation. That leaves us with—' I tripped over a purple stone jutting out of the orange grass, skinning my knees and palms.

But the plenties finally stopped walking away. Instead

they all glared down at me on the ground. 'There's no need to act like a buffoon. We'll stay.'

My heart soared in my chest. 'That's great. Thank you.' I spied a few more plenties outside the pod. 'You go ahead and get yourselves settled. My colleague and I are just going to speak to some more people.'

Of course, by the time we got back a few minutes later, they'd all left.

BB walked up behind me. 'I don't see how we're going to get everyone off the planet in time.'

Just then I saw Rincy waddling our way. For a second I wondered where Aurora had gone – but then I spotted her. She was mostly a sort of coral-red hue, which made her hard to see amongst all the, er, orangery.

Bexley galloped up to them. 'How'd it go at the civic centre? Were you able to talk to Bob? Did she have anything more to say?' Her energy astounded me.

Instead of speaking, Rincy flopped down onto the ground like a discarded bear rug. Well, more of a platypus rug.

Holly took the opportunity presented by that slight pause. 'An unknown caller is requesting to speak with you,' said Holly. 'Shall I put her through or decline the call?'

'An unknown caller,' I repeated. 'Hang on, everyone. I have to take this.' I moved away from the group to seek a modicum of privacy on the far side of the getoff. 'Yes, please. Put her through.'

Bexley waved at one of her tall, pointed ears. It seemed she was getting the same call.

'Hello,' said an unfamiliar voice.

'Hi. Are you...' I wasn't sure what to say next. It felt like I was making it up as I went along. 'Are you the person we've been waiting to speak to?'

'I believe so,' said the voice. Holly translated all speech into human-sounding voices, so I had no way of knowing whether I was speaking to a kobold or a plenti or a sentient tree. For all I knew it was a computer reading a pre-written message.

'That's amazing,' Bexley said. 'Thank you so much for agreeing to speak to us. We're enormously grateful for your time.'

I took a breath. 'Is there somewhere we could meet? We'd like to speak to you. In person, I mean. Have you got a place we can do that?'

There was a pause. Like the person on the other end of the line was making a difficult decision. Or maybe she was typing her reply. No idea why I thought that – but I did. 'I will meet you – but please understand how big a leap of trust this is. My people do not trust the usurpers.'

'Thank you,' Bexley said. 'We will not abuse your trust – I promise. You have my word.'

Another pause. 'Sadly, we've heard that before too.' Her words were flat, tuneless. 'My conditions are non-negotiable. Are you ready to hear them?'

BB, Aurora, and Rincy all stared intently at us. 'Yes, we're ready,' I said. 'Please go ahead.'

'Thank you.' Her voice was closer to the one Holly used for itself than the ones it assigned to people. 'I will meet with one of you alone. You may not bring anyone else or tell anyone where the meeting is. You must bring no knives or weapons of any kind. And lastly, the meeting place will be chosen by me. Are these terms acceptable to you?'

'Oh, come on,' cried Rincy. 'What's she saying?'

I made a wait gesture – though I had no idea whether she would understand it. The second condition the kobold placed on the meeting – the one about no one knowing where the meeting was – worried me. But I didn't think we had much choice. We needed to get through to them.

I looked at Bexley. She tapped her hooves in the air.

'Okay,' I said. 'We agree.'

'Thank you for that. I know I'm asking you to take a leap of faith.' Another pause. 'But my people have learnt not to trust. And that knowledge has been gained through hard experience.' The voice was still flat, uninflected. Holly always picked up on people's intonations – I wondered why it wasn't getting any this time. *Maybe I was right and the words are being typed?*

Bexley looked me in the eye. 'We only want to help. I promise.'

The caller disregarded that. 'When you have decided which one of you will meet me, I'll text that person the location.'

'We'll discuss it and send you a message,' I said. 'And thank you again.' Rincy was dancing from foot to foot. Aurora glowed bright turquoise.

'And remember what you have promised,' said the mystery caller.

'We will,' said Bexley.

The moment the call ended, Aurora, BB, and Rincy all practically pounced on us with overlapping questions.

'What did she say?'

'Have they agreed to meet you?'

Bexley and I took turns recounting the conversation.

'Oh my gosh,' said Bexley. 'Do you know what this means? There's no way someone could hold down a conversation like that if they weren't a mature sapient!'

I smiled at Bexley's limitless enthusiasm for life. Which – fascinating though it was – meant we really were dealing with an oppressed people. I forced the panic back down. We had to help them.

'Alone? No, no way,' said Rincy. 'Not alone.'

I nodded – a thoughtful sort of nod, not agreement. Not that any of them understood human body language – although I supposed their translators would probably make something of it. 'I get it. And I understand your concerns. But I don't get the sense we have anything to fear from the kobolds. And besides, whichever one of us goes, our AI will know where we are. If anything happens to us, it'll alert everyone right away.'

They weren't thrilled. But since we didn't have much choice, we all agreed.

———

In the end, it was me who went. I was instructed to meet the mysterious caller at the Museum of Dave, at the building's rear entrance, near the rubbish bins.

Spock rang as I was walking. I pulled out my phone and accepted the call. 'Hi, sweetie. How are you doing?'

She was lying on the bed in our room. 'Lem? Where Lem?' From her perspective, my image would appear on the screen on the wall.

'I'm down on the planet,' I said. 'I'll be a few more hours. Are you okay? What have you been up to?'

She leapt off the bed then turned back to grab her toy brain. She hurled it at me – well, at the screen where I appeared. 'Lem play.'

'I can't play right now. I'm on the planet Dave, remember?' Of course she didn't. Her short-term memory was a few minutes at best. 'The one with the kitties.'

She stood up on the bed, ears forwards. 'Eat tasty

kitties?' To be honest, the temptation to let Spock chase the plenties was strong.

I arrived at the front of the museum. 'No, they're not for eating. Anyways, sweetie. I have to go. I'll see you in a few hours.'

'Not come now?'

'No, Spock. Not now.' I peered around the edge of the purple two-storey building, looking for a way to get to the back. 'I'll see you as soon as I can. Bye.'

When she lay back down on the bed, I ended the call. I followed a narrow pathway around the edge of the building. The rubbish bins were right where you'd expect them. It looked like they were still being emptied regularly.

I glanced around, trying to make sure I stayed out of sight of the road, assuming my mysterious caller picked this spot so we wouldn't be seen. After a few moments, the museum's back door opened and a small creature came out carrying a bag of rubbish.

It was the first time I'd had a chance to look at a kobold properly. She stood not even to my waist – looking like a tiny pachycephalosaurus. Her legs were large in proportion to the rest of her, though not as big as her tail. Her scaly skin was mottled, blending various shades of green and blue. She motioned for me to follow her behind the bins.

Sticking with my alphabetical naming scheme, I decided to call her Dinah.

When we were alone, she set down her bag. 'Hello. Can you understand me?' Her mouth didn't move, but her little hands flew.

'Hi. Yes, I can.'

'Thank you for agreeing to my conditions.' Her voice sounded like the same one I'd spoken to earlier – but now with inflections and varying tones. Like a person's voice rather than a machine.

For a moment I wondered about the new layers to her intonation. It added weight to my theory that she'd been typing earlier when we talked on the phone. She didn't seem to be speaking aloud this time either – and yet her words were imbued with inflections and a more natural rhythm.

She continued. 'I'm sorry I have to be so secretive – but if I'm caught, my life will be forfeit.'

'Your life,' I repeated awkwardly. 'Forfeit? What? How?' *And they say you can judge a species by its ability to convey coherent thoughts.*

With her pudgy face and large eyes, she looked young. 'I am lucky that my ... that the person who keeps me doesn't treat me as badly as some do. All kobolds in Catford are kept by plenties. If I am caught with this translator, I will be sent to the detention centre. The only kobolds being evacuated are those who are brought by the plenties who keep us. We must choose between slavery and death.'

My hand shot up to my mouth. 'What? No, Dinah. That isn't how it works. We're here to evacuate the planet before it's destroyed. That means everyone. You do *not* have to go with the plenties. Not one of you has to go with them. You don't have to travel with them or stay with them. Your removal from this planet is not conditional on the plenties.' It had only been a few months since I'd left Earth and discovered there was any such thing as a Galactic Union – but I knew this much for certain.

It was her turn to resort to spluttering. Well, hand sign spluttering. 'What? No, they told us you wouldn't take us. That they'd had to fight for the right to bring even some of us. They said if you found out we could use language, you'd cancel the entire mission. It's been all over the kobold news forums.'

Pinching the bridge of my nose, I said, 'I promise we wouldn't do that. Why would we?'

'We're a complication,' she said. 'An extravagance. And you don't want to become embroiled in unnecessary drama. And they said you have policies against *lesser* species.'

My head tilted to one side, that same gesture Spock made when she was confused. 'But you're people.'

'No, we're not.' Her eyes narrowed as she looked at me. 'Well, that is … we think we are. But they – the plenties, I mean – tell us we're not.'

For some reason, I thought back to my first encounters with non-Earth species. It had taken time to adapt to all the many different types of people I'd met. 'How could you not be people?'

Dinah disregarded my question. 'So, you'll really take us with you?'

'Of course we will. We don't want *anyone* to die here. And we don't want you to be exploited either. None of you have to go with the plenties to their new home if you don't want to. We'll work with the GU to find you your own home world somewhere else if that's what you want.'

'What?' She sounded sceptical. 'But where would we go?'

I shrugged. 'I don't know. Anywhere. We'll work with the government. That is, *you'll* work with them. I mean, we'll support you.'

Her eyes were wide. 'And you won't hurt us? Won't leave us here to die? Not even if we say we want to be independent of the plenties? Aren't you worried about the trouble we'll cause?'

I wanted to cry for her people. But that wouldn't help.

'No. Our only job is to get you – all of you – safely off this planet. Where you go after that is up to you and your people.'

She took a deep breath. 'What about the free kobolds? The ones who don't live in Catford?'

I had no idea what I was getting myself into here, but leaving people to die wasn't an option. 'Yes, them too.'

Her hands were still as she seemed to consider this. 'Okay. Will you do me one more favour, please? It's small – I promise.'

Inside I was praying I wasn't going to be made a liar. But I smiled. 'Sure. What is it?'

She looked up at me. 'Visit the museum and pay close attention to the section called the *Founders' Story*. When you've finished, return to your colleagues and tell them what we discussed. I'll go to my people and try to persuade them the truth of what you've told me. Four hours from now, I'll send you co-ordinates. Bring no more than three others and meet us there and you can explain to the council of elders.' She looked towards the back entrance. 'I'm already late. I have to get back before anyone notices I'm gone.'

After Dinah left me, I wandered in through the front entrance. The museum's four rooms each housed a different exhibition. Holly read the signs to me as I looked around.

The Founders' Story was all about the establishment of the colony on Dave – 400 years earlier. A few exhibits appeared to be preserved sections of one of the generation ships they'd come here in. Or maybe they were replicas. Whatever. The bridge or cockpit or whatever you want to call it fascinated me. It looked like something out of *Star Trek* or *Firefly* – but so much smaller than I expected. It must have been a scale model replica rather than a relic. No way could full-grown plenties have sat in those seats.

I shuddered when I got to the mockup of the ships' living quarters. Similar to what we had on the *Teapot*. But these were generation ships – people would have lived their whole lives on board. Imagine living and dying on a crowded space-ship, never setting foot on a planet or seeing the sky above your head. Never feeling rain on your skin or the warmth of the sun. I thought about the people who'd lived here – only for their descendants to have to abandon their new home a few hundred years later.

Suddenly I felt a need to escape – to see the sky above me. I had no clue what Dinah wanted me to see. My muscles unclenched when I stepped outside. The sun felt warm on my skin as I walked back to the evac site with a new sense of purpose.

———

Another getoff launched just before I arrived back at the pod park. Seeing it fly was like watching a shipping container being sucked up by a giant invisible vacuum.

Bexley was due for a break. We sat down with Rincy in the park next to the evac site.

As I chewed on a meal bar, I told them about my meeting with the mysterious Dinah. Both Bexley and Rincy were aghast when I told them about the kobolds' belief they'd be left to die.

'I mean Bob is – let's face it – pretty awful,' Bexley said, 'but surely she wouldn't tell a sentient species they'd be abandoned on a planet with no escape from certain death. Would she? I mean, I don't like her. But she wouldn't do *that*, would she?'

Rincy declined the food we offered but opted to sit with us while we ate. 'After how she behaved when we went to see her this afternoon, I wouldn't put much past Bob. She has no love for the kobolds.'

Swallowing a mouthful, I nodded. 'Yeah, she straight up told me I had mistaken a bit of mimicry for genuine speech. But Dinah is highly articulate. There's no way that wasn't genuine.' I squinted as a thought occurred to me. 'Actually,

I'm pretty sure they don't speak with their mouths – so Bob's argument doesn't even make sense.'

Bexley tossed her mane over her shoulders – or tried to. It was too short to be an effective move. 'Wait, what? How do you mean? Like, they're telepathic? I didn't think that was a real thing.'

'No, I mean she uses a form of sign language.' I made a vague speaking motion with my hands. 'Hand signals.'

Rincy plucked a blade of orange grass from the ground and studied it. 'Then how did you hear them earlier?'

'I guess...' I bit my lip. 'Huh. I don't know. Maybe they sometimes speak aloud or...' I crossed my legs in front of myself. 'Hey, Holly?'

'Yes, Lem. How can I assist you?'

I looked up at the turquoise sky. The clouds sparkled like they were filled with glitter. This planet was so ridiculously beautiful. I'd have to remember to take some pictures before ... well, before everything. 'Earlier today, when I overheard the kobolds speaking... That is, when you translated their conversation – do you remember that?'

'I do,' Holly replied.

'Right back,' I said to the others. I stood up and wandered a few metres away so I could focus on Holly. 'How did you hear their conversation?'

'I did not,' said Holly.

The vast majority of the time, Holly made my life a thousand times simpler and clearer than it would otherwise be. But every once in a while, something reminded me it was just an idiot chatbot. 'You translated their conversation for me, Holly. How were you able to do so?'

'I saw them speaking,' it replied. 'And I thought you would be interested in what they were saying. Should I not have done so?'

I reached out to touch the grey bark of a tree. It was softer, smoother than it looked. 'You were definitely right to do so. Thank you. I'm just trying to figure some things out. Are you confirming the kobolds use some kind of sign language? Not a verbal one, I mean.'

'That's correct.'

I chewed my lip. 'Okay, cheers. And how were you able to see them when I couldn't?'

The voice in my ear replied, 'You hadn't consciously noticed them, but they were within your line of sight.'

I scrunched up my face. 'They were?'

'Peripherally, but yes.'

'Thanks,' I said. 'But they can understand speech – well, at least the one I met could.'

'They appear to hear well,' Holly said. 'When you spoke to Dinah, her translator conveyed your words to her in Persian.'

One eyebrow shot up as I smirked. 'Persian, huh?'

'It seemed like the sort of pun you might like,' Holly replied. 'If you're not happy with my choice, you can —'

'Nope. *Purrrrrr*-sian it is.' I bit my tongue. If I succumbed to the giggles now, I might never recover. The human mind is a weird thing. 'Anyway, cheers.' I strolled back to where BB and Rincy were sitting and told them what I'd learnt.

'None of it changes the fact they're sapient,' said Rincy. 'Bob was patently lying to us when she said otherwise.'

The ground in front of Bexley was littered with crumbs from her meal bar. 'Yeah, no, for sure. We'll have to talk to that government minister again – the one overseeing this mission. There's no way we can be part of making the kobolds stay with the plenties. Was Dinah their leader?'

I sat down on the ground next to Bexley. 'I don't think so.

She seemed young. And she wasn't sure anyone would believe her.'

'Who will you take with you?' Rincy asked.

'Us three? I suppose if the place we're meeting them is outside Catford, then Spock could come, right? She could really use the outing. I feel bad for her, being cooped up on the *Teapot*, while we're all down here.'

Bexley reached out and touched my knee. 'She'd like that. That's a good idea.'

Rincy did a sort of push-up onto her centre arm. 'I can't join you, I'm afraid. My responsibility is here.'

My arms fell by my side. 'What? No. How can... I can't... What?'

Bexley, who had several months' worth of understanding my gibberish, said, 'How can we speak on behalf of the GU? I have a reasonable understanding of what the law says – but I don't feel comfortable committing to what resources and support they'll actually provide in the next couple days. You're in charge of the mission, Rincy. Like, what if we make promises they won't keep? If the kobolds ask what we will and won't commit to, you're the only one here who can answer that.'

Rincy flopped down onto her belly. 'What do you want me to do, Bexley? We're supposed to be twenty per cent of the way through this evacuation. Instead we're getting further behind with every passing minute. The plenties may be awful. And they are – they're horrible people. I don't like them one bit. But they don't deserve to die. Even if I thought they did deserve to, I'd still be duty bound to do everything I can to prevent it.'

She pushed herself upright and waddled a few steps towards me. 'I can't do everything – I just can't. My job is to evacuate the plenties. I trust you – both of you – to do the same for the kobolds. Whatever you tell me we should do ... that's what I'll recommend. I'll support you and I'll provide you with any resources I can. But we have to get *both* groups safely off this planet before that asteroid arrives.'

Bexley knelt down and wrapped her arms around Rincy. 'I'm sorry. I should have seen how much pressure you were under.' She looked up at me. 'We can do this, can't we, Lem?'

I took a deep breath. 'Yeah, we can. You two are off shift now. Go, get your rest. I'll join the others getting people to load these getoffs for the next few hours. When I hear from Dinah, I'll ring you both. One way or another, we'll get it all done.' At least, I hoped we would.

———

The next few hours were an absolute slog. We sent the crew from the other ships back out into town to urge people to join us. Plus, we were still dealing with protesters. For every two people we persuaded to leave the planet, the protesters convinced another to stay behind.

Aurora and BB worked at one getoff while Henry and I managed the other. According to the original plan, we should have launched another four getoffs before Dinah's call. We were all but forcibly chucking plenties into the transporters and tying them down. We didn't do that, obviously – but it did feel like that was the only way we'd get the mission accomplished before the deadline. The actual *dead* line.

Most of the projects I'd managed had hard due dates – but never *this* hard. No one dies if an IT project wraps up a few days late. However much the client may act like it.

Eventually, Holly announced, 'Dinah is requesting to speak with you on a visual channel. Shall I put her through or decline the call?'

I gestured to Henry that I needed to step away. 'Put her through, please, Holly.' I pulled my phone from my pocket.

The line crackled with static as a miniature Dinah popped up on my phone. 'Hello? Are you there, Lem?'

'Hi, Dinah. Thank you for getting back to me.' I leaned against the wall of the pod, grateful for the brief respite. It was cool in the shade.

'I've discussed the situation with my … the elders of the community.' She paused like she was struggling to find the right words. 'They've agreed to allow up to four of you to come here to discuss whether you can help evacuate any of us.'

My heart broke for her. She still thought we were going to abandon them. 'Dinah, I promise, we will not leave you or your people here to die. Not if you want to leave.'

Dinah ground her teeth. 'They will not go with the plenties. I mean, they don't want to travel with them – but they especially want to be sure we'll be resettled together – far away from the plenties.'

'We can make that happen.' I *really* hoped I could keep that promise.

'I will send co-ordinates to your device. It will take you about two hours to walk here. Do not send your vehicles here – not until you've agreed it with the elders.'

Two hours? How far away were they? In this gravity, we could easily walk at least ten kilometres in that time. Catford was only about one kilometre wide.

'Hang on… Won't it be getting dark soon?' I asked.

Dinah looked puzzled by the question. She touched her chin. 'No, not for another few months. I have to go now. Call me when you're getting close.' She cut the call.

I headed back for the getoff. 'Henry, I've got the co-ordinates.' I tried to call Bexley, but she and Spock were already in the transporter on their way back down. Since Rincy was staying in Catford, I asked Henry to join us.

———

Spock was delighted with all the new things to sniff at and pee on. I kept her on lead, though, as she still wanted to bark at every plenti she saw.

Mind you, so did I. The arrogant bastards.

'Hey,' I said. 'When I was speaking to Dinah earlier, I asked if it would get dark soon. But I think something got lost in translation. Do either of you know when nightfall is? We're going to need Henry's big lights if we're walking in the dark.'

'No,' Bexley said as we passed a turquoise and red striped apartment block at the edge of town. Well, it looked like an apartment block. 'Dinah's right. Dave's days are longer than its years. It's so cool, actually. It spins really slowly on its axis – which means they have four seasons: dawn, day, dusk, and dark. We're nearing the end of the day season now.'

'Huh.' We fell back into a comfortable silence – except for Henry, whose silences were always as hostile as her words.

We passed a few farms as we walked. The sun glowed a warm red overhead. The clouds I had seen earlier had disappeared. Orange grasses ran right up to the edge of the purple road. On the horizon, lavender mountains rose to touch the turquoise sky.

'The planet Dave is so beautiful,' I said. 'Don't you think?'

Henry stopped rolling forwards. 'What do you know about it, sandwich? How many planets have you even been to?'

I scoffed. 'Plenty! Five.' Spock stopped to sniff some of the orange grass.

'Um,' said Bexley. 'I think we might have a problem. Like, I don't mean to interrupt your fascinating conversation —'

'No, six! I forgot to include Earth.' *Oops, that just burst out of me.* 'Sorry, go on.'

Bexley glared at me. But then she shrugged – a gesture she'd picked up from me at some point over the last few months. 'Anyways, like I was saying, I think we've got a problem.' She pointed to where the road ended about twenty metres ahead of us.

Spock strained on the lead as she tried to go off exploring. 'What? I don't see anything,' I said.

'Cup,' said Henry.

'The road ends,' said Bexley.

'Yeah, I see that,' I said. 'But it doesn't look so bad. I'm glad I've got sturdy shoes, but it looks doable.'

Henry spun in angry circles on the road. 'Oh, it looks frolicking doable, does it? The three of you can walk just puffing fine, can you? On your meat-legs. Well, that's jolly nice. For you.'

The reality of what she meant hit home. 'Where we're going, there are no roads.' I put my hands on my hips. 'Who puts stupid little plastic wheels on a service robot anyway? What's even the point of that? Who designed you? Did your people not have stairs or uneven ground or rocks?' It was awful and unfair of me. I was stressed and I lashed out – but that was no excuse.

'You're going to talk to me about the inefficiency of *my* design? You, sandwich? Are you even kidding me right now? Your body once tried to kill you. Have you even had a look at yourself? How much RAM do you have? How fast is your processor? And why do you need so many lumps and bumps and holes? It's disgusting. And what's that sound you always make? It's like *splorp*. My software doesn't even dignify it with a translation.'

'Yeah, anaphylaxis is no fun.' I scowled at her for a moment, trying to puzzle that one out. 'And splorp? Do you mean sneezing?' I shrugged. 'Actually, yeah. Fair play. I could do without so much sneezing.'

'You could do without so much running your cobbing mouth,' replied Henry.

To be fair, I couldn't disagree with that. I shouldn't have said what I did.

Bexley waved her arms. 'But what are we going to *do*? Henry can't travel over the uneven ground. And no, I'm not going to suggest we carry you. Besides, we've got almost ten kilometres to go and even in this pathetic gravity you're freaking heavy.'

'Nice try, fur-brain. But I'm going back. You three carry on without me. I'll get back to corralling the parking plenties into the pods. Truck, maybe if I mimic Spock's approach to them, the bollards will move faster.'

Before I met Henry, I'd never given much thought to accessibility. I really should have.

We all wandered to where the road ended and looked out over the land spread out before us. Low, rolling orange hills were dotted with purple rocks and plants that were unlike any I'd seen anywhere else under an aquamarine sky. Every so often, there was a cluster of trees – with their grey bark and leaves in every shade of peach, orange, gold, and coral.

After a moment of admiring the view, Henry revved her motor and rolled away. 'See you whenever, meatsacks.'

'Bye, cranky friend,' called Spock in response.

Bexley looked at me. 'I guess we'd better get a move on.'

I tapped my fists in the air. We set out in search of the free kobolds, leaving the last traces of Catford behind us.

'Hey, Henry,' I shouted.

She rolled to a stop about twenty metres back the way we'd come. 'What?'

'I'm sorry.'

She waved some sort of flag at me as she wheeled back to town.

———

When we were well away from Catford, I let Spock off her lead. Bexley sometimes dropped to all fours and ran with her, exploring the new territory. The pair of them probably covered twice the ground I did with all their wandering off and circling back.

'How much further, Holly? Surely we've gone way more than ten kilometres already,' I said for the gazillionth time. I was ready to collapse.

'You are less than fifteen metres from the edge of the kobold city,' it replied.

'No, that can't be right.' I stopped walking. 'Hey, Bexley. Holly says we're basically there. I don't see anything. Do you?'

Bexley stood beside me. We looked around – me shielding my eyes to get a better view and her sniffing the air.

Spock took off running. 'Spiky friends!'

'Spock, no,' I called in desperation. 'Come back.' But she didn't listen. Bexley and I ran after her. I didn't think she'd see the kobolds as prey the way she did the plenties, but I didn't want her to spook them. They were already fearful of us. One wrong step – or bark – on our part could doom these people.

I was so busy focusing on Spock that at first I missed the kobolds popping out of their tents. *Wait, tents?*

And just like that I was standing in the middle of a city I hadn't even noticed. Small kobolds of varying hues of green and blue ran from the tents to hug and pet Spock.

Larger kobolds emerged and began shooing us. 'Away, away, get out,' translated Holly. I wasn't sure which person's words she was interpreting, but it didn't seem to matter. They were all saying the same thing.

Bexley and I raised our hands and backed away from the group. 'Spock, come. Come here now,' I hissed through clenched teeth.

Spock didn't come. But then, no one seemed to be telling *her* to leave.

A lone kobold ran towards me in a sea of kobolds running the other direction. 'Lem, what on Dave are you doing? You were supposed to call me before you got here. Why didn't you? Ugh. Do you even know how hard it's going to be to undo—'

A tall, thin kobold ran up to Dinah and wrapped her arms around her protectively. After a moment she released Dinah to free her hands. 'What are you doing, Dinah? Who are these people? Have you led them to us? I only just got you back. Why would you risk the safety of our community?'

Dinah turned to face the person – her parent, I assumed – giving her every bit as much reproach as she'd given me only a moment earlier. 'This is Lem. I told you about her. She's the one who's come to help us free ourselves from the plenties. And to get us off this planet before the asteroid hits. They're here to help. I *told* you.'

But the protective parent gave as good as she got. 'Yes, Dinah. We did speak about this. And you know full well what we decided.'

Suddenly feeling incredibly awkward about this whole thing, I glanced around. More than a dozen small kobolds clustered around Spock, all begging for their chance to stroke her. A few others were creeping towards Bexley or me, daring one another to touch us. More worryingly, dozens – possibly hundreds – of larger kobolds peered out of tents that blended in with the orange and purple landscape.

Dinah's parent looked up at me – though a few centimetres taller than Dinah, she still stood to about my waist. 'Well, I guess you'd better come with me.'

All eyes were on us as we followed Dinah and her parent across the settlement, which I dubbed Drumheller.

The tents were a camouflage fabric, seamlessly blending shades of purple and orange. Almost impossible to see in a landscape dominated by the same two colours.

'Spock, come.' She reluctantly complied.

There were way more tents than I would have guessed. This wasn't just a camp; it was a city. *How many people are there? What have we got ourselves into? How are we going to evacuate everyone? Do we even have enough ships?*

Dinah's parent led us to a tent and lifted the flap. 'In. Now,' she signed. The interior of the space was warm but smelled significantly better than any tent I'd ever been in. It was open to the sky, so it was also much better lit than my experience of tents. Since the space was too low for me to stand upright, I squatted.

Dinah's parent – sticking with the alphabetical theme, I decided to call her Elim – glared at her child. 'Tell them to sit.'

Dinah glared right back. 'They *can* understand you, you know.'

Elim turned to face Spock. 'I'm sorry – I didn't know you could sign.'

I squat-waddled towards Spock, trying to put myself in Elim's line of sight. 'No, I'm sorry. We can't.'

Dinah poked her parent's shoulder, re-directing her attention to herself. While signing, the pair kept their feet touching.

'Dinah is interpreting your words for Elim,' said Holly in its own voice. 'Would you like me to translate her translations back to you?'

'What?'

'Dinah is interpreting –'

'No, I meant "what?" in a surprise sense, not a– You know what, just never mind. No, do not translate my own words back at me.' I looked up to find everyone staring at me. 'Sorry, sorry. Elim, I assume you're Dinah's parent. Is that correct?'

Once Dinah had interpreted my words, Elim signed back. 'I am her house-parent, yes. How do you know Dinah?'

I nodded. 'We' – I indicated Bexley and myself – 'said we wanted to speak to a representative of your people to co-ordinate the evacuation. And Dinah was the only person brave enough to come forwards.'

Elim studied Dinah's face. 'My brave, foolish child!' She faced me again. 'Dinah trusts everyone too easily. She has no awareness of the danger she places herself and those around her in. That's how she was taken in the first place.'

Dinah set her face into a stern expression. 'I am well aware of danger – surviving with the plenties the past three years has made me more aware than I would wish on anyone.

But I'm *trying* to be brave in spite of my fear. Because if we do nothing, our people will die.'

'Well, I guess you have learnt something since I last saw you.' Elim leaned to rub shoulders with her child before facing us. 'As an adolescent, she wandered too far from home and the poachers snatched her. I didn't see her again until today. For the most part the plenties ignore our city. But every few months or so, they send hunters out – mainly taking those who stray from Drumheller.'

Elim turned back to me. 'Now tell me why you are here – and quickly. The council of elders will not want to be kept waiting after Dinah's flagrant disregard for the rules. Even now, they will be planning to disassemble the camp.' The words were harsh, but as she signed, her feet stroked Dinah's affectionately.

Bexley and I alternated speaking as we explained the dire urgency of the evacuation as succinctly as we could.

Elim's powerful tail quivered. 'So our choices are to stay here and die in a few days – or to be evacuated with the plenties and to surrender our freedom forever.'

Bexley and I both blurted, 'No!'

'Never that,' I vowed. 'When we arrived, we were told that your people were...' I wasn't sure how to finish that sentence, but I had to. As I shifted to a sitting position, I bonked my head on the ceiling. The tent wasn't actually open to the sky. It was clear like glass but moved like cotton.

I motioned for Spock to come to me. 'This is my dog. She is sapient but not ... mature. She relies upon me for her care in much the same way a child relies upon her parents.' I stroked her head. 'When we first arrived, Bob told us your people were like Spock – dependent on the plenties.'

'Spock good girl?'

I smiled at Elim then looked at Spock. 'Yes, you're the bestest girl.'

Elim's tail swished in faster, smaller strokes. 'Why would you believe such egregious lies?'

Bexley pushed her forelock down over her long nose. 'We hadn't met you ... any of you. We didn't know. Taking the plenties' word for it was wrong. We were wrong. I'm so sorry. But we want to put it right.'

Elim pressed her elbows towards one another – like crossing her arms over her chest but still leaving her hands free to sign. 'By enslaving all of us?'

'No, that's what we're trying to say,' I said. 'None of you has to go with the plenties.'

'We can relocate you separate from them,' Bexley added.

'So we can be enslaved all over again by the "supremacy" of mouthspeakers.' I could practically hear the air quotes – Elim's words dripped with all the scorn Holly could fit into a simulated voice.

Something finally clicked in my brain. 'That's their justification for saying you're not sapient!' I slapped my forehead. 'It's because you use sign language.'

Dinah stopped translating for her mother and looked directly at me. 'Yes, I thought you understood that.'

'I'm sorry. It wasn't obvious to me.' How had I missed that? And what a pathetic excuse for denying the peoplehood of people who were plainly, well, people.

Dinah continued signing for her parent while I considered the implications.

Bexley put a hand on my knee. 'No, Elim. That's what we're saying. You can go anywhere you want. Well, anywhere that has room for you. If you don't want to go to the same planet as the plenties, no one will make you. There are so many different species in the galaxy – thousands upon thousands. And the GU doesn't get everything right. Not by a long shot. But one thing is absolutely clear in every law I know of: no one race has the right to oppress or enslave another. Slavery is *never* allowed.'

Dinah asked her to pause so she could catch up. After a moment she nodded to Bexley to continue.

'So, I don't know. Like, maybe a planet that's home to other, um, handspeakers. Or one where you'll be alone. Or whatever. My point is, there are options. *So many options.*' Bexley held her hoof-hands out towards Elim. 'But it's up to you to choose.'

Elim pursed her already flat lips. 'This is' – her hands rested calmly in the air in front of her for a moment – 'not what we expected you to say. But then, how do we know we can trust you?'

'I guess … you can't know.' I gripped the back of my neck – suddenly aware that any movement of my hands might be interpreted as having meaning which could undermine my words. How would I know? 'But you have two choices right now: believe us or don't. If you accept what we say, we'll take you off this planet before it's destroyed. If you choose not to believe us or you don't consent to evacuation, that asteroid will hit this planet in about sixty-five hours. If you don't come with us, well… This beautiful planet isn't going to be very nice. I don't pretend to understand the science of how things will change. But I know that even *if* anyone survives, they'll be left to eke out a living in an inhospitable environment.'

Elim looked away from her child – her eyes dropped to the rough purple ground beneath us. 'The council of elders are aware of the threat. We have made –'

'You what? You knew?' Dinah gawped at her parent.

'You knew this planet was doomed and you didn't do anything? You didn't tell anyone?'

Both kobolds stood there, their hands silent.

At length, the tent flap was pulled back and a new face looked in on the group. The newcomer looked at Elim and then signed, 'Oh, wow. She wasn't lying – the big one is weird looking. It's like her body can't decide whether to grow fur or not. And the one with the nose ... she must be capable of smelling the stench of Catford from here.' She reached out a foot to stroke each of our feet, pausing when she got to Spock. 'This one is lovely, though. Is she their leader?'

Elim glanced at me, her eyes sparkling with mischief. Well, I *thought* it was mischief. She looked back at her friend. 'They can understand you, Fenchurch.' Holly had clearly cottoned on to my ingenious naming scheme. '"The big one" and "the one with the nose", as you so eloquently describe them, speak for their people. The beautiful one is their child.'

Close enough.

Fenchurch's mouth opened and she flushed almost indigo as she looked at Bexley and me. 'Forgive me, I merely came to tell you the elder council is waiting.'

'It's quite all right. Most of my shipmates have said similar about me.' It was true. They had – all except Bexley.

Fenchurch looked from my face to my hands and back again. For a moment I thought perhaps I'd inadvertently made an offensive gesture.

But then Dinah poked Fenchurch's arm. 'The mouth-speakers have translator devices that tell them what you've said. And I have one that translates their words into Persian. But you'll have to rely on me to interpret.' She turned to look at me. 'The kobolds in Catford understand Persian, but even here there should be a few survivors who do. Do you have more devices for them?'

Bexley and I looked at one another. 'I... We...' I stammered. 'Sorry, we should have brought some. We will next time. If we're invited back, I mean.'

———

Fenchurch and Elim led us to the large tent where the elder council met. I could stand up – barely. Like the first one we'd visited, the top was transparent, making the space well-lit.

Eight kobolds sat in a circle. Everyone budged up to make room for us. Dinah sat between me and Bexley to continue translating. Spock lay on the ground in front of us.

Bexley and I repeated everything we'd just told Elim.

There didn't appear to be any one leader, so we spoke in a way that addressed each of them in turn. Of course, their eyes were mostly on Dinah as she interpreted.

'If we believe you,' said one, 'and we haven't yet voted on that, so it's still very much conjecture – but if we believe that you will not deliver us all into the hands of the plenties, what will become of our people? Where will we go? How can you ensure we won't be oppressed and taken advantage of all over again?'

I looked at Bexley. She, having grown up a citizen of the GU, knew more about how things worked. 'Our first priority is to get everyone,' she said, 'both kobolds and plenties... Well, and anyone else who happens to be here as well. I don't know if there are any other species living here or in Catford – but our mission is to get everyone safely off the planet before that asteroid hits. Once people are out of immediate danger, we'll look at what comes next. But I can tell you this – what the plenties have done to your people is illegal. They will not be permitted to continue or to do it again.'

Dinah tapped her on the elbow. 'Hang on. Need to catch up.'

'Oh, sorry,' Bexley said.

When Dinah finished interpreting, she gestured for Bexley to carry on. 'Where was I? Sorry, right. So, once we get everyone safely off the planet, then we'll talk about who will go where. The plenties are going to Phoebe station for now. It's in the process of being built and the builders have agreed to lease it to the government for a few months while they work with the plenties to find a long-term home for them. But, um, well, like I said… What the plenties have done to your people is against galactic law.'

Bexley emphasised each word with gestures. She paused again to let Dinah catch up. 'Okay, I have to preface this by saying I'm not a lawyer or anything. I know a little bit – and one thing I know for certain is that protecting people from slavery and oppression is a core tenet of the GU. So there will probably be a trial. Bob and the other leaders of their government will have to take responsibility for what they've done to you. If they're found guilty – and I'm assuming they will be – then the most likely outcome is that they'll have to make reparations to you and the leaders will be sent for reha-bilitation. My guess is the entire population will have to undergo some re-education. It may even be made a condition of their resettlement.'

Dinah's hands flew as she repeated everything for the elders. Bexley's words were translated into English for my ears almost instantaneously. Having to wait for a second layer of interpretation slowed things down. It made me appreciate Holly all the more – and hope we could get some AI units that made visual translations.

Mind you, I didn't need an interpreter to pick up on Fenchurch's hostility. While the rest of the elders sat in relaxed positions with their faces neutral but attentive, Fenchurch held herself rigid. She crossed her arms in front of herself protectively.

'Again – not a lawyer,' Bexley said. 'But I know for certain … well, like, not much really. But no one will force you to do anything.'

A thought occurred to me. 'How many of your people are there? In your city, I mean?' My shoulders fell. 'Wait, is there only one kobold city? Or are there others?'

They looked at one another. After a few moments, one of the elders – not Elim or Fenchurch – answered. 'There are approximately two thousand of us here. And as for our number in Catford, perhaps our young friend here can enlighten us.'

Two thousand? How the hell were we going to cope with an extra two thousand people in the next two days? We barely had enough ships and getoffs for the residents of Catford. And now we had to accommodate half that again. It wasn't as if there was any wiggle room on the deadline.

Everyone looked to Dinah for an answer. She raised her hands and then lowered them. And then tried again. She blushed a deeper blue. 'Er, I think… That is, I've heard…'

Elim waved at her child, getting her attention. 'It's okay, Dinah. No one expects you to know the precise answer. Just give us your best guess.'

Dinah took a deep breath. 'I think there are about three hundred.'

One of the others looked at me. 'Can you accommodate us?'

Swallowing the lump in my throat, I said, 'I'll be honest. We can't promise much of anything. This mission was pulled together in the last few days. The plenties… Well, they rejected the scientists who told them this was coming. They only contacted the GU about a week ago. It's taken this long to pull it all together. It's not going to be easy.'

Fenchurch uncrossed her arms – though her posture remained just as closed off. 'Why should we take your word for any of this? For all we know, you may have made a deal with the plenties to load us onto your ships and take us away from our home and sell us into slavery on alien worlds far and wide.'

I couldn't blame her for her scepticism. 'You know we're not lying about the asteroid, right? Elim mentioned that much earlier.'

Fenchurch narrowed her eyes. 'We are not ignorant. But that doesn't change anything. There's still nothing to convince us you're not working with the plenties.'

My brain was running a million miles a minute, trying to come up with something to offer to persuade them we were genuine. 'We might be able to arrange for you to speak with the GU Minister for Refugees. Would that set your minds at ease?'

'Another mouthspeaker, I presume,' growled Fenchurch.

'Enough, Fenchurch,' said Elim. 'You will get a vote – same as the rest of us. But at some point, we have to trust people.'

Bexley exhaled noisily. 'I *promise* you we will do every-thing we can to get you safely off this planet and away from the plenties – even if it means we'll all be crowded into ships like hay in a bale.'

It wasn't until after she'd finished speaking that I realised the elders were all looking expectantly at Dinah. After a moment, she flushed blue. 'Oh, er… Sorry, Bexley. I forgot I was supposed to be translating. Can you repeat that for me. Sorry!'

Poor Dinah. She was holding up way better than I would have. It was easy to forget that she was just a teenager.

Bexley repeated what she'd just said.

One of the elders stood up and crossed her arms over her chest. 'So you're saying you'll prioritise the plenties over us? Their safety is your primary concern?'

Bexley and I both replied, 'No' at the same time.

At this outburst, Spock – startled out of her slumber – jumped to her feet. 'Rude.' She circled around a few times and then lay back down.

Around the circle, everyone signed at once. Holly couldn't translate them all simultaneously – or perhaps it simply knew I couldn't parse them all. But it did feed me snippets.

'… mouthspeaker supremacy…'

'… all the same…'

'… think they're better…'

'No,' I repeated. 'Absolutely not. We only mean that we started with them because we had no idea you were here. We will do our absolute best to transport as many of both groups as possible, even if it means we're all packed in like —' I couldn't think of how to finish that sentence without sounding like I was hyperbolising. 'No matter how tightly we have to squeeze in to make it work.'

Bexley brushed her forelock down over the shaved remnants of her horn. 'We absolutely do not subscribe to the theory that the plenties are in any way superior to you. I know they tell you they are … but I disagree entirely.'

She chewed on nothing while Dinah finished translating that. It was a thing Bexley did when she was trying to think. 'I'm … different to most of the people on my world. We don't need to go into details, but suffice it to say, I'm a bit of a unicorn.' I doubted she'd actually used that word – she *despised* that word. It was more likely that Holly had translated her words figuratively. 'And people look down on me for it. They say it makes me less, it makes me inferior. But it doesn't. I know that's what the plenties want us to believe – that your differences make you inferior. But you're not.'

Another pause while Dinah caught up. 'If I had to choose, I'd side with your people over theirs any day. I think you're about a gazillion times nicer. But our job is not to be the arbiter of who is more worthy – it's simply to save as many lives as possible. Because no one – and I mean no one – has a greater right to life than another. That's why we're here and that's what we're going to do.'

I put my hand on her shoulder. She didn't like admitting her unicorn-ness to anyone.

'Look, I don't know if we can get everyone off this world before the asteroid hits.' There was a pleading tone to my voice. 'I don't know if there are any other ships we can call in. And I don't know where you're all going to go after this. But I promise you—' I was trying so hard not to let my hands do any speaking, but I found myself holding them out in front of me, willing the kobolds to understand. 'I swear, we will do everything in our power to get every last one of both groups off this planet before the end.'

'Dinah,' said Elim, 'please take our guests to the community centre. A meal is being prepared. They will need food and rest.' She turned to Bexley and me. 'Thank you. We will consider your words. We appreciate your candour. Once we have voted, we will come find you.'

Dinah led us through Drumheller, with Bexley babbling excitedly as we walked. Now that we weren't rushing, I had more time to look around.

People gawped at us. I'd grown used to standing out in crowds – even as a shortish human, I was usually taller than the various other species we encountered. Bexley stood to about my shoulders and the rest of the *Teapot* crew were shorter than her. Well, except Aurora. Her physical form, such as it was, was amorphous. And, as always, the fact I wore clothes made me stand out even more.

A crowd of kids appeared from in and behind tents, all looking to take a turn stroking Spock.

When we'd passed through the warren of tent streets, we arrived at an open area. A hundred or so kobolds sat at low, wooden tables. There was a pleasant hubbub of people cooking, serving, eating, drinking, and socialising. But it still felt oddly silent to me.

All conversation stopped as we approached – which is to say, everyone's hands fell to the table. At the centre of the space stood a couple of large, low brick ovens and pots hanging over open fires. Several people were cooking, weaving past and between one another with a grace that surprised me. I'd have thought their massive tails would get in the way.

Since I'd woken up this morning – after just three hours of sleep – I'd been through the ringer. Herding cats, accidentally discovering a mature sapient species, a meeting with a hostile government, secret meetings, a two-hour hike, a meeting with a slightly less hostile government. If I didn't get some rest soon, I was going to crash. It occurred to me I was probably hungry too. I should eat first. No, we had to talk to Rincy. I could feel an indecision loop coming on.

'Dinah,' I said. 'Bexley and I should check in with our team. Is it okay if we rejoin you in a bit?'

She held her arms out to the sides. 'Sure.' She backed away as she signed. 'Come find me when you're done. I'll save you some seats.'

I wanted to lie down – right there on the pale purple ground – and sleep for a week. 'Come on, Spock. You stay with us.'

We wandered a few metres away. Not having to worry about mobile signals was the best thing about the future. Not the future. Outer space. I mean, not space. We were literally on a planet.

Whatever.

I dropped onto the ground. 'Holly, can you put me through to Rincy, please?' Bexley sat next to me and took the phone from my faltering hands. She held it flat and extended the camera attachments, aiming them at both of us. Spock lay down beside me.

'Of course, Lem,' Holly replied.

A tiny hologram version of Rincy appeared, standing on top of my phone. She was juggling bags and boxes, trying to balance them all in her webbed hands. 'Bexley, Lem! How are you? How's it going with the kobolds?' She lost her battle with the parcels – they tumbled around her. One rolled towards Bexley and me. I was too exhausted to even flinch. But it disappeared before it fell off the edge of the screen.

After another round of greetings, Bexley and I took turns filling her in on what had happened since we left Catford. My eyes were like lead weights.

Rincy picked up a bundle of bags. 'Honestly, I don't see how we're even going to get the plenties off the planet in time. These people just refuse to co-operate.' She flung several of the packages she'd only just picked up back down on the ground.

'If the kobolds agree to evacuation,' I said, 'and I hope they will, then I have a feeling it will run more smoothly.' Beside me, Bexley tapped her hooves in the air.

Rincy dropped what she was holding. 'Hey! What do you think you're doing?' She must've run because the camera tried to show us every direction at once. Mostly turquoise sky and orange leaves. 'No,' she bellowed. 'Get away from that!'

A little tree grew out the face of my phone where Rincy's image had been a moment ago. Presumably she'd dropped her device with the camera facing up. The sounds of various textures rustling filled my ears. Bexley and I looked at one another. We both shrugged and waited for Rincy to come back. Although the situation was dire, in that moment there was nothing we could do.

'*I said* you get away from that,' Rincy repeated. 'Are you seriously trying to wreck the getoff? We're trying to evacuate your people.'

We couldn't see her or whoever she was speaking to – still just that tree – but a new voice replied, 'This is our home!

You have no right to force us to leave. We won't stand by and let you get away with this.'

'We're not forcing anyone to go anywhere. But this planet is going to be destroyed. If you stay, you will die. And so will your children. Don't you want a future for them?'

Eventually the plenties must have wandered off because Rincy shouted, 'That's right! You go ahead and leave. I can get back to helping people who want to live.' She muttered incoherently. 'Are you kidding me right now? Where did everyone go? You there, did you see the people who were sitting in these seats?'

I looked at Bexley. 'Er, I think she's forgotten about us,' I said.

'Lem? Lem? Is that you? Are you here?' I imagined Rincy spinning around in the getoff looking for me.

'Still out in Drumheller, Rincy,' I replied. 'I think you dropped your tablet somewhere. We've got an image of a tree instead of you.'

'Oh right, right, right.' We could hear her moving around. 'Where ·was I when we were talking earlier? Okay, if I just retrace my steps…'

My eyes drifted shut.

After a few – whatever, however long it took – she appeared on the phone again. 'Sorry, I'm so sorry. Anyway, where were we?'

'The kobolds,' I said.

I leaned on Bexley as she asked, 'How are we going to get them off the planet before the asteroid hits?'

'Honestly,' said Rincy, as she bent down to pick something up off the ground, 'I've kind of got my flippers full here. We're so far behind. According to the schedule, we should have loaded about fifteen hundred people. We've not even done half that. I've been calling in crews from the various transport ships to try and round people up – but the plenties have no sense of urgency. And I've never met a more disorganised group.'

Which, if you thought about it, was pretty funny coming from Rincy. Or maybe it was all the more meaningful. She knew all about disorganisation.

She stopped fiddling with whatever it was she was holding and looked directly at us. 'I trust you. Your whole crew. I'll let the minister know to expect your call. She'll support you in any way she can.' Rincy's image disappeared.

It felt like all the steam was forced out of me. I just … deflated. Bexley rubbed my back.

After a couple of minutes, Spock wagged her tail. It was that particular wag of a dog who's excited but too tired to do anything about it. 'Spiky friends.'

I lifted my head to see Dinah and a few others trying to look casual as they walked towards us. 'Hi. Are you finished with your meeting? These little ones wanted me to introduce them to Spock, if that's okay.'

'She's pretty tired,' I said. 'But if you're very calm and you approach one at a time, I'm sure she'd love to meet you. Briefly.'

The kids formed into a neat queue and approached when it was their turn. When someone had questions, Dinah patiently translated our responses.

I typed a message for Bexley's eyes only: CAN WE GET ENOUGH GETOFFS? AND SHIPS?

Bexley looked at the ground and muttered aloud, 'We'll figure it out.'

Dinah led us to the area where everyone was eating. Once again, hands stilled as we approached. People stopped eating and drinking and moving – meaning the silence got even, er, silenter? Quieter, that was the word. The noiselessness was so complete it felt like my ears had been stuffed with peanut butter.

The tables were laid out with serving bowls and platters laden with different kinds of food. I didn't recognise any of it. But I was pretty sure it was food. Dinah stopped and gestured to a table near the centre of the space. Three kobolds – young adults if I wasn't mistaken – sat there already and there were four more vacant seats.

'Please join us,' said one of the people. 'We have sufficient food to share.'

'Oh, er,' said Dinah. 'I don't know if you can eat our food. I hope so.'

'It's okay,' said Bexley. She pulled a little device – like a tricorder crossed with a smartphone – from the holster she wore around her waist. 'I can use this to check.'

There were lots of oohs and ahs from everyone at the table – expressed both audibly and in handspeak – as Bexley clicked a few buttons and a sort of needle-probe emerged from one end of the device.

'See, with this,' Bexley said, 'I can check the chemical composition of the food.' She inserted the probe into one of the dishes and waited a moment while it analysed the findings. 'This one is safe for all of us. It might be a bit spicy, and the protein complement is on the low side for Spock, but it won't do any of us any harm and will meet at least our short-term needs quite nicely.'

'Feed Spock?' Drool pooled under her snoot.

'In a minute, sweetie,' I reassured her. 'Wait.'

Spock sat down and swished her tail in anticipation. Bexley repeated the process with the other dishes on the table. Our companions were fascinated.

Something occurred to me. 'Do you eat the same things as the plenties?'

'Mostly,' said one of the kobolds. 'We come from the same home world, so it makes sense that our biologies would have evolved to be similar in many ways.' She helped herself to the food from one of the bowls and then passed it widdershins to the person next to her.

Bexley and I looked at one another. 'Both the kobolds and the plenties come from the same planet originally?' I asked.

'Well, yeah,' replied Dinah. 'That reminds me... What did you learn when you visited the Founders' Museum?'

The person on my left passed a bowl to me – full of what looked like bright blue roasted carrots. I scooped some of them into two bowls: one for Spock and one for me. 'Well, if I understood what I saw, then the plenties – and, I guess, your people too – have been on this planet for around 400 years. The voyage was made using generation ships, so it seems faster-than-light wasn't an option. I'm not sure how long the journey took, though.'

The next bowl came my way as I passed the first to Bexley. It was loaded with a brightly coloured stew of some sort. The chilli scent shocked my nose.

'Yes,' said Dinah – apparently relishing the opportunity to play teacher. 'And what did you learn in the cockpit?'

While I tried to call up the memory of the cockpit in my mind, I added helpings from a third dish – turquoise berries – and set Spock's bowl on the ground. 'Er... It was a scale model replica.'

Dinah touched her chin. I'd noticed that sign a few times. It seemed to be handspeak for 'no'.

Carefully, I tried the food. Once, as a child, I'd eaten caustic soda. This felt like that. Although the jewel-toned dish had a consistency like stew, it tasted like a chemical fire.

When I stopped coughing, I spluttered, 'It was a replica, wasn't it?'

Spock sniffed her food and then pushed the bowl away. 'Evil.'

Bexley took a giant spoonful of her stew – I was about to warn her when she rammed the whole thing in her mouth. 'Oh, my gosh! This is amazing.' Huh. Maybe the salted grass dishes she favoured were more than they seemed.

Dinah swallowed her mouthful of stew and looked me in the eye. She set down her spoon so she could speak. 'What makes you say that?'

I balanced my spoon in my hand. 'Well, it wasn't big enough … that is…' The truth slapped me in the face. I let out a long, slow breath. 'It wasn't sized for the plenties – it was sized for the kobolds.'

'Now you're getting it.' Dinah picked her spoon back up and ate quickly while she had a moment's peace.

I tried the other dishes – just the tiniest droplets of each. All three had different flavours and textures, but each one was spicier than I'd ever encountered. My mouth was blistering.

Bexley smacked her lips noisily as she sampled each of the foods in her bowl. 'The spice is hotter than I'm used to, but the range of flavours is divine.'

One of the others at the table nodded. 'Thank you. I was part of the team that prepared this evening's feast. I'll pass your compliments along to my fellow chefs.'

I looked around the open air dining area. 'So, it was the kobolds who flew the generation ships. Not the plenties.' They cooked over an open fire. I hadn't noticed any artificial power since we'd been in Drumheller. No electric lights. No communication devices. They had running water, but it operated by handpump.

'That's right,' said Dinah. 'I was taken before I finished my education. But my friend here is specialising in our people's history.' She indicated the person to her right.

This was all fascinating, but I desperately needed a nap. No, I needed a two-week holiday. But I'd settle for six hours of sleep.

'Oh, that's amazing,' said Bexley. Indefatigable Bexley. 'I love learning about history and cultures. All the different ways people develop and advance. How cultures evolve. What they consider important or sacrosanct or taboo. It's all just so amazing, don't you think?'

Poor Dinah had to set her spoon down in a rush to try to keep up with what she was saying. I didn't envy her the task of repeating Bexley's words when she got going. Bexley spoke about a mile a minute and changed topics on the fly. I loved her, but trying to translate for her – anticipating where she was going – would be a challenge for even the most advanced interpreter.

Before I knew it, the meal was finished and the conversation was flowing freely.

Bexley gently shook my shoulder. 'I'm awake,' I cried. Looking around, I was startled to find that the dishes had been cleared away and most of the people had left. If we'd been on most planets, I got the distinct impression it would be dark and the manager would be asking us to move on. Spock was lying on her back, one leg twitching in the air.

Stroking my long hair, Bexley said, 'I had Aurora send pods for us. I'm going back to Catford to help load the getoffs. You and Spock are going to the *Teapot* to get some sleep. You're no good to us if you're not functioning properly. And we all need to be at our best. Aurora suggested we get in touch with Gracie. If the *Pequod* is still in range, they may be able to help with the evacuation.'

I rubbed sleep from my eyes. 'Oh. Yeah, that's a good idea. I mean, those are all good ideas.' With a yawn, I added, 'Hey, did the elder council vote yet?'

She tapped her hand-hooves in the air. 'Yeah, they want to live. They want the chance to be free for more than a day.'

Although I was relieved to hear it, I couldn't get my hopes up yet. I nodded. 'Now we just have to figure out the logistics.' My body sagged as I exhaled. 'How long until the pods get here?'

She stood aside, revealing three blue phone-box pods a few metres away.

I'd be in my own bed in less than an hour. 'Bexley, have I told you lately how much I love you?'

She grinned as she helped me to my feet. 'Yeah, but you can say it again anyways.'

Holly startled me into wakefulness by singing Nirvana's 'Smells Like Teen Spirit' at me at full blast.

Spock fell out of bed and glared at me. 'Rude.'

'I'm not getting much sleep this week, eh?' I grumbled.

'Adult humans are advised to get eight hours of sleep per night,' said Holly unhelpfully.

'Shut up, Holly.' I rubbed sleep from my eye. 'That was a rhetorical question.'

Holly shut up.

Even with almost eight hours of sleep, I was still struggling. My body clock was all out of whack. By shipboard time, it was three in the morning. I plodded into the bathroom and did what I went to do. A few minutes later, Spock and I trudged our way to the kitchen.

Bexley greeted us with a warm smile.

Spock was her usual self. 'Hello, talky-friend. Feed Spock?'

'Of course, I'll feed you, you silly muffin. I've got your breakfast right here.' Bexley lifted the lid off a bowl of nutrient porridge. The mouth-watering aroma of sweet potato vindaloo filled the air, setting my stomach rumbling. She set the bowl on a serving tray, which she hoisted and carried through to the mess.

We followed her. Spock did a very pretty sit, her tail swishing happily on the floor.

Bexley set Spock's bowl down in front of her then turned back to the tray. 'I wasn't sure what to make for you, Lem. Last night I said to myself, "Well, you're not getting a breakfast order out of her." I mean, you fell asleep at the dinner table while I was talking to Dinah and her friends. Your little mouth was open and you were leaking all over the table. It was kind of adorable and only a little gross.'

Heat rose in my cheeks. 'Oh no. What must they think of me? I feel so bad.'

Bexley handed me a mug of steaming purple helbru. 'What they think of you is that you're an organic being with needs and limits. They think you're not a perpetual energy machine that exists to serve.'

I grimaced. 'Yeah, but I couldn't even stay awake until dinner was finished. It's so embarrassing.' I blew on the helbru and then breathed deeply of its floral scents.

'Nonsense,' replied Bexley, waving off my all-too-human shame. 'Now, as I say, I didn't get a breakfast order from you, so I was racking my brain trying to remember what your go-to foods were and I couldn't think of anything and I was getting really ... anyways, whatever. So I set it to create something random from your preferences file.' She lifted the lid off the second bowl on the tray.

The delicious scent of coconut reached my nose. 'Oh, that's perfect. I love you.'

I dropped to one of the dining chairs to enjoy my meal. Luckily, it was a coconut and raspberry chia pot. A lot of my favourites were quite spicy. But my lips and tongue were still burnt from the kobold meal last night. 'Whatcha pa fuh uh-uh?'

Bexley's ears swivelled like little satellite dishes trying to catch a signal. 'Um, sorry. My translator couldn't make out any of that. Was it something important? Because maybe you should—'

Waving her off, I swallowed the mouthful of creamy yet tangy nutrient porridge. 'Sorry, I said – well, I tried to say – what's the plan for today? We should set up a call with the government minister and we should check if Gracie's still in the region. And then I guess it's back down—'

Bexley waved her hooves in the air. 'Oh that. Yeah, no, we're all good. Aurora did all that for us. We're speaking with the minister in' – she paused to check the time on her pendant – 'a quarter of an hour. Henry's waiting for us in Ten Backwards. And then after that, we've got a holo-call with Gracie. When we finish that, we'll sit down to sketch out the details of the kobold evacuation. By then it'll probably be lunchtime. While we eat, we'll agree our schedule of who does what when.'

I waved my last spoonful of porridge-flavoured porridge at her. 'Look at you, Captain Organised.'

Bexley smiled proudly. 'I know, right? Check me out.'

———

'What's up, meatsacks?'

'Morning, Henry,' I replied as Bexley, Spock, and I walked into Ten Backwards. 'How's it going down on the planet?'

Henry extended what looked like a dentist's mirror and examined her spotless body. 'Those fluffy werecats are a menace to civilised society. They make even you look competent by comparison.' And then just to make sure I didn't mistake that for a compliment, she added, 'And you set the bar so astoundingly low I keep tripping over it.'

Rolling my eyes, I dropped heavily into the chair sized for me. Spock curled up under the table and went to sleep. I considered joining her. Bexley sat next to me.

'Everyone ready?' asked Henry.

I had no script and no idea how to phrase things. Having never met directly with a government minister before, I wasn't sure what the protocol was – not that my Earth-based knowledge would be of any use even if I'd done that sort of thing regularly. 'What are we supposed to say?'

'Just be honest,' Bexley said. 'She's a person just like us. It's the facts she cares about. I'll get the conversation rolling.'

'The kobolds are pickling doomed if you two are the best the galaxy can come up with to get them off the guacamole planet.'

Bexley waved a hoof dismissively at Henry. 'Shush, you. It's time to start the call.' She clicked a button on her tablet and the same peri we met a few days previous blinked into existence. Her colouring was different to BB's. BB was mostly gold – with jewel tones under her wings and on her head. The minister, by contrast, was a vivid royal blue with spots of fuchsia and yellow visible when she lifted her wings in greeting.

She appeared to be sitting in the same leafy, green space she'd addressed us from before – but this time it was dark.

I took a moment to count primes silently while I pushed my anxiety to the back of my mind. 'Good morning, Minister.'

'Yes, I suppose it is morning,' she replied. 'Somewhere.' There were only a few small lights – like candles – dotted around her.

'Hi,' said Bexley. 'I'm so sorry for disturbing your sleeping period. We definitely wouldn't want to do that if the matter weren't so pressing. You see, we're orbiting the planet Dave, assisting Rincy in the—'

'Yes, yes, I've been briefed on the status.' The minister fluttered her wings – an impatient gesture I'd seen BB use on occasion. 'The evacuation of the plenties is proving more of a challenge than anticipated. And now you've discovered a second mature sapient species and they're in need of removal as well. The asteroid will collide with the planet in just over two days and the current resources are insufficient to the task. Have I covered the salient details?'

I winced.

'Yes, Minister,' said Bexley.

The minister clicked her beak. 'Can anyone tell me how in the hell the plenties failed to notice that there was a whole other species living alongside them?'

'They didn't,' I began at the same time as Bexley said, 'Well, that's the thing—' I searched for the best and briefest way to say it.

The minister crossed her lower set of hands over her waist. 'You, cylindrical one. Can you be more succinct?' I thought about how cranky BB got when she had less than twelve hours of sleep.

Henry wheeled closer to the holo-camera. 'The plenties are well aware of the kobolds. However, they deny that they're mature sapients—'

'Doesn't matter.' The minister ground her beak. 'Whether they're mature sapients, immature sapients, or mere sentients, the fact is they're people – beings who are capable of sensing and feeling. We cannot and will not abandon our duty. The implication that the plenties may be urging us to do so will be investigated and dealt with. But first we have to get both peoples off the planet safely. They have my full support. Whatever resources you need, I'll sign off. Just get them to safety.'

I decided to press my luck. 'It also appears the plenties may have enslaved kobolds.'

The minister pulled her wings tight to her body and ground her beak. 'Yes, Rincy mentioned this disturbing news. I assure you, the matter will be thoroughly investigated and dealt with accordingly. But first … get everyone safely off the planet.'

I released the breath I'd been holding. All three of us thanked the minister.

She clucked a final time and winked out of existence.

I leaned back in my seat. 'Well.'

Henry extruded something that looked like a feather duster. 'Filching well.'

Bexley crossed her arms on the table in front of herself. 'Filching well, indeed.'

We sat in silence – punctuated only by Spock farting contentedly in her sleep. Our meeting with Gracie wasn't due to start for a few minutes. Even though Bexley and Henry both needed less rest than I did, we were all shattered. The only one present who hadn't been pushing herself too hard for several days straight was the one asleep under the table.

Out of nowhere, Bexley clapped her hooves. 'Oh my gosh, Lem. I forgot to tell you what happened overnight. There was a massive catfight. Someone in one of the getoffs decided she'd rather be in the other getoff. She made dozens of people move from one getoff to the other because she and her family absolutely had to be in the right one. It took hours to switch everything out.'

My jaw fell slack. 'The *getoff*? She wanted to travel in the other getoff? Did you not tell her the trip was only eighteen minutes?'

Henry flipped down a spatula of some sort and jabbed me with it. 'Gee, pancake. Shame we didn't have you there to think of that for us.'

Bexley swatted at Henry. 'Shush. Be nice to Lem.'

'I am nice. This is me being frolicking nice.' She retracted the spatula.

'Anyways,' continued Bexley. 'Guess what happened when they finally finished swapping everyone out.'

I breathed in slowly. 'They didn't. Tell me they didn't.'

Bexley swung her too-short mane back over her shoulders. 'Oh, they tried. Said they needed to switch everyone back. Henry slammed the door and told the pilot to take off before anyone could move.'

'They lodged a cuffing complaint too,' said Henry.

Bexley snorted loudly. 'Did they? You didn't tell me that part.'

'I swear, these plenties are going to be the death of us.' I looked at my watch. 'I think it's time for our meeting with Gracie.' The *Pequod*'s captain's refusal to participate in the mission a few days ago was still a sore subject.

For the second time in less than a week, I flinched as a wall of water appeared in the room with us.

'Well, what is it?' barked Gracie by way of greeting. If one could be said to bark when one's words were rendered in a sing-songy voice by a universal translator, that is. Gracie was shaped like a whale or a tardigrade. I still couldn't find a face.

'Um, good morning, Gracie,' said Bexley. 'Thank you so much for agreeing to meet with us. We're aware you were unhappy with the plenties' reluctance to be guided by science and that when it was revealed that they'd delayed the evacuation by several years already…'

Gracie flapped her – were those legs or flippers? – whatevers – impatiently. 'Skip to the end.'

'Captain Gracie,' I said as crisply as I could. 'Yesterday we learnt of a second species on planet Dave. They're mature sapients but they don't have advanced tech. They knew about the asteroid, but had no means of doing anything about it.'

Gracie wiggled in her pool. 'What do you mean they couldn't do anything? Explain.' She waved a flipper-leg at us. 'Briefly.'

'Ooh, yeah.' Bexley jumped back in. 'It's so interesting, actually. I was speaking to one of their historians last night and it seems that while the kobolds aren't super technologically advanced, they used to be – even more than the plenties. They originated on the same planet, right? And there was this group of kobolds who felt that their reliance on technology had cost them their connection with nature. They wanted to find their own planet to start over, living a peaceful existence in tune with their environment.'

Gracie swished her flipper-legs. 'Get to the point, mouthspeaker.'

Something registered in my brain. But I couldn't quite grasp it.

'Right, okay, um, so…' Bexley pushed her mane over her shoulders – only for it to flop back down where it started. 'They brought some of the plenties with them to their new home. The two species had always lived in a sort of symbiotic harmony, but somehow after they landed on Dave, the plenties—'

'Mouthspeakers,' I blurted.

I hadn't meant to speak at all. But I certainly didn't mean to be so loud.

Spock jumped up and glared at me. 'Rude.'

Gracie blinked several of the eyes along her torso. 'Pardon?' Or were those mouths? Vents?

Bexley's ears stiffened. 'What? Are you okay, Lem?'

Henry waved a maybe-dildo at me. 'As much as it pains me to say this, the mouthspeaker is right. The plenties said the kobolds weren't sapient. Their justification was that the kobolds don't speak – but the truth is that the kobolds are highly articulate. Only they speak with their hands, not their mouths. The plenties—'

'Mouthspeaker supremacists,' roared Gracie. Muscles rippled beneath her skin.

Henry extruded a pair of chopsticks and jabbed one at Bexley and one at me. 'Hah. Tell me about it.'

Bexley glared at Henry. 'Shush, you.'

I nodded. 'That's exactly what they are, Captain. Not only have the kobolds been oppressed and enslaved by the plenties, but now their lives are on the line. All because they're the victims of mouthspeaker supremacy.' I only had one chance at this. 'Please. Help us help them.'

Gracie swam a somersault in her tank for an endless minute. 'For mouthspeakers, your team aren't half bad, Henry. We will help the kobolds. But I will not have any of these plenties on my ship.'

'Thank you, Captain Gracie. Thank you.' I breathed a heavy sigh.

Bexley pushed her forelock down. 'That's fantastic. But um… How quickly can you be here?'

Gracie appeared to consult with someone outside the camera's range. 'My team are plotting our course now. Travelling at maximum warp, we should arrive in just under four hours. Will that be sufficient?'

'We'll need to see your specs,' I said. 'Specifically the speed and capacity of your getoff. Can you—'

'I'll get them to you now.' Gracie and her tank both winked out of existence.

Henry wheeled out of her seat. 'I've got the specs.'

I drained the last of the helbru from my mug. Ugh, cold Marmite flowers. 'Shall we head back to the mess? We can put on another pot of helbru and get comfy while we plan the logistics.'

'Ugh, you can keep your weird purple uppers,' said Bexley. 'But you've sold me on the comfy seats.'

The door whooshed open and Henry rolled out. 'You meatbrains are weirdly obsessed with physical comfort. I'm going back to the bridge. Patch me into your conversation if you need someone with a functioning CPU to do your thinking for you.'

———

I saved my work on my phone once I was satisfied with the data. 'Okay, so assuming the loading and unloading go smoothly – *a lot* more so than with the plenties – it should take us less than two days to evacuate the kobolds. Twelve hours to spare. They're smaller than the plenties, so the *Pequod* can accommodate most of them. We should be able to take a hundred kobolds on the *Teapot*. It'll be cramped and uncomfortable – but it's doable.'

Bexley chomped down on her fourth hay biscuit of the morning. 'We'll give our quarters up for the six days it'll take us to get to Deep Space Five. We'll all be camping out on the floor of the lounge on the bridge deck. Do you think BB and Aurora will be okay with giving up their room for a few days?'

I massaged the back of my neck. 'They won't like it any more than we do – nor will Henry, for that matter – but they'll understand. No one's going to prioritise their privacy over the kobolds' lives.'

Bexley opened her mouth to reply, but a new voice interrupted. 'Lem? Are you there? You can't keep ignoring me like this. Don't you even know who I am?'

Unfortunately, I did know who she was. 'Bob, how did you get this number?'

Bexley's jaw fell open. She mouthed something in her own language that was presumably whatever her name for Bob was.

'As you know,' Bob said, 'we agreed that you could bring as many of our kobolds as you could fit on the ships that were already orbiting Dave. That did not give you the right to take an entire day off to go hang out with the feral ones outside the city. How dare you! What do you have to say for yourself?'

Bexley stood up and tried to ask me questions.

'Bob, you told us the kobolds weren't sapient. You tried to prevent us from even finding out about the group at Drum—'

'Silence,' roared Bob. 'I will not tolerate such gross insolence from my staff. Lem, you and your team will report to the evacuation site immediately. No excuses. My people are the priority here. You will—'

I waved a hand in the air, metaphorically pushing Bob's voice away. 'Holly, reduce Bob's volume to minimum.' The prime minister's tirade continued but softly.

The door to the mess swished open and Henry wheeled in. 'Hey, cheese brains, I'm getting an unauthorised transmission. Have you heard anything?'

Bexley galloped over. 'Bob seems to have hacked into Lem's comms. I think she's shouting at her.'

Henry rolled to a stop. 'What the blondie badgering book? How did she get through without permission?'

Bexley and I both shrugged. 'She's discovered our plan to evacuate the kobolds,' I said. 'Suffice to say she isn't happy about it.'

Henry rolled in a tight circle. 'And she does know we won't let it impact the evacuation of the plenties, right?'

Scrunching up my face, I replayed what Bob had said so far in my mind. 'Good question. Holly, turn Bob's volume back up for a sec, please. And can you relay it to the others as well?'

'… paying the cost of this evacuation, which means I pay your salary and if you think for one —'

'Bob.' I began hesitantly but picked up confidence as I spoke, knowing I wasn't alone in this. My instinct was to fire off a witheringly sarcastic rant but I worried that – while it would be cathartic – it could have horrible repercussions for the kobolds. 'I assure you that our arrangement with the kobolds has nothing to do with the plenties. Just because a few people have been reassigned to focus on the kobolds shouldn't be taken as a sign that Catford is being abandoned. Rincy and her team —'

I winced as Bob's reply brought a fresh assault on my eardrums. 'I know full well what the implications are. And I hope you know that I am personal friends with the GU Minister for Refugees. She will not take kindly to your gross effrontery. Leaving the pleasure doll in charge of a rescue is not a suitable option.'

I mouthed the words, *pleasure doll*? My companions couldn't have known what I said but Bexley shrugged and Henry flapped two wing-like appendages.

'All attempts to evacuate kobolds will be abandoned this minute.' Bob's voice rose to a fever pitch. If there had been any glass in the room, I'd have feared for its structural integrity. 'From now on, no kobolds will be permitted to board—'

I bit my tongue. 'Holly, hang up on her. I'm not going to listen to that anymore.' I feared for the safety of the kobolds if I upset Bob more than I already had — but if I had to listen to her anymore, I wasn't going to be able to bite my tongue.

'I'm afraid I can't do that,' it replied. Bob was still bellowing. 'Would you like me to dim the volume again?'

'Yes, please. Thanks, Holly.' I slapped my hands to my forehead. 'Henry, can you figure out how to end this call, please? I'm not ... I just ... I can't.'

'Not that I'm in the habit of taking orders from a guacamole meatsack — but in this case, I'll make an exception. She's hacked in pretty deep, though.' She rolled out of the room. 'I'll be on the bridge. If I have to, I'll disconnect that entire node.'

Shaking my head, I tried to breathe out my tension. 'Wow. That was different.'

Bexley looked up into my eyes. 'She's really taken off the mask, eh? So much for the magnanimous leader we met a few days ago.'

In the background, Bob continued shrieking and wailing. She made threats against me and us and the kobolds — both the ones in Catford and the ones further afield.

Bexley flared her nostrils and sniffed the air. 'I'm worried about retaliation. What if the plenties take out their anger at us on the kobolds?'

Running my hand over my head, I counted primes to quell the turmoil in my mind. 'Agreed. We need to get every kobold out of Catford and away from the plenties. They're not safe. Holly, can you call Rincy for me, please?'

'I'm sorry, Lem,' Holly replied. 'Not until the current call is terminated.'

Bob's tirade finally faded as Henry's disembodied voice said, 'Got it. That plucker won't be able to get back in without your express permission. Little bollard. Right, if that's all, I'm going back to my recharging dock.'

I sighed. 'Yeah, cheers, Henry. I owe you one. I'll see you when you're done charging.' Looking at Bexley, I added, 'Once we've called Rincy, we'd better get back down to Drumheller.'

I fell asleep in the transporter pod. That's like falling asleep while skydiving. It wasn't until Bexley pulled open my door to check I was okay that I woke up. Spock barked excitedly and danced in circles.

'Jeepers, how long was I out?'

Bexley shrugged. 'Not long. I only just got out of my pod. I opened Spock's door for her and then came to get you.'

I stepped down and gave Spock a quick pet. 'Right. We need to meet with the council of elders as soon as possible. They have to get packing.'

'That shouldn't be an issue,' said Dinah.

I spun around to face her. 'Morning. You mean the elders are ready to see us?'

'They are,' she said. 'But that's not what I meant. Come, follow me.'

Dinah led us through the city to the council's tent. Except the city wasn't there anymore. About half the tents were gone. A few were being pulled down as we passed. The land was filled with kobolds beavering away, disassembling everything. One family worked together to roll up the walls of a tent. Children ferried boxes and bags. Well-muscled individuals pulled up enormous tent pegs.

Though no one spoke audibly, the work was far from silent. People grunted with the strain of effort. Fabric made soft kssshing sounds. Wooden pieces bumped together to make low-pitched noises. Metal clanged.

Dinah pulled back the flap on a still-standing tent. 'The council of elders is waiting.'

'Thank you.' We emerged into the warm light of the tent. The elders were all in their seats. The four of us – Dinah, Bexley, Spock, and me – sat down in the space left for us. 'Oh, er, before I forget… We brought more translators.'

Several of the elders looked at one another. A couple of them laughed awkwardly. 'I assume these are auditory devices?'

I nodded. 'Yeah, they translate from one language to another so you— Oh.' I bowed my head. 'I'm sorry – I'm missing something, aren't I?'

Bexley's nostrils flared as she sniffed the air.

The same person, not someone I knew, replied again. 'We don't know any mouthspeaker languages. Not well enough to rely on such a device at any rate. I myself recognise the Persian words for *yes* and *no*, numbers as high as five, and a wealth of different curse words. But I doubt that will be much use in organising the logistics.'

Another elder said, 'I was captured as a child. It's been many years since I escaped, though I should still be able to understand some Persian – though most of it would relate to things you find in a kitchen. I doubt it would be useful to our discussions here.'

'Ah.' I felt incredibly stupid.

Elim smiled kindly. 'If I understand correctly, your devices translate by bonding to an individual. Unless you've brought enough with you this morning for everyone with even the smallest understanding of Persian, we'd be better off saving them for the people who have the most complete understanding of the language. Thank you.'

'Well, we're glad someone will be able to use them,' said Bexley.

I have so much left to learn about how the universe works.

'I take it you have come to us with news,' said Elim. 'What is the verdict? Have you been able to arrange transport for our people?'

'We have,' I said. A collective sigh of relief echoed around the room. 'For all of you.'

Most of the kobolds touched their right hands to their chests. 'Thank you.'

Fenchurch clenched her jaw. 'And what guarantees can you offer us that you are not working in conjunction with the plenties to enslave those of us who have so far remained free?'

I opened my mouth and then closed it again as a thought occurred to me. 'Actually, the captain of the ship that's coming to collect most of your people shares your low opinion of mouthspeaker species. When she arrives, you can discuss your concerns with her.'

Most of the other elders turned to look at Fenchurch.

'Thank you,' said one – her hand on her chest. 'Fenchurch, will that reassure you?'

Fenchurch narrowed her eyes. 'We don't know this species or who their allies are. And they aren't here to sign for themselves. We only have these mouthspeakers' word for their attitude.'

Elim shook her head. 'You know the choice we face – either we go with them or we die.'

'But the caves,' said one of the other elders. 'We'll take refuge in the caves.'

'Enough,' said another. 'If you want to trust your future to the caves on a dying planet, go ahead. We will miss you. But you were outvoted.' She turned to face Bexley and me. 'We began packing everything up last night after you left. Although we hoped you would come today with news that you could accommodate us, we also had to be prepared for the alternative. There are some caves. If you hadn't succeeded in securing ships for the evacuation – or if you hadn't found places for everyone – we would have gone there in the hope that some of us would survive.'

In my mind's eye, I envisioned whole families sitting together in the dark – clutching one another as they waited for their world to be torn asunder. I shook my head to clear that depressing image away. 'Well, I'm pleased it won't come to that – for whoever chooses to join us at any rate. We've drawn up a plan for the evacuation.'

'Yeah,' said Bexley. 'If your people are as organised at boarding the getoffs as they are in disassembling your city, we should have you all off the planet's surface with time to spare. In fact, I think it's likely you'll be done before the plenties. Even though they've had a head start, they're proving to be, um…' She chuckled nervously.

To my surprise, most of the elders replied to this audibly. It took me a few moments to recognise it for what it was. Laughter.

'I'm sorry,' said Elim. 'You must think it churlish of us. But we have a saying. It predates the migration to planet Dave – from when our two species lived together in harmony. Well, *mostly* in harmony. *Herding cats*. It is a reference to how wilfully stubborn and independent they are. Trying to get a group of them to co-operate together on anything is ... it's a challenge.'

I smiled broadly. 'My people have the same saying. At least, my translator conveys it using the name of a species of immature sapients from my planet. They ... well, yes. They can be a handful.'

'I am glad we see hand-to-hand,' said another elder – confusing me briefly with her mixed metaphor. 'How will the evacuation be organised? When do we need to be ready?'

I dropped my arms and crossed my hands behind my back, hoping that wasn't considered rude. 'We've persuaded the captain of a large transport ship to come to your aid.'

Bexley fidgeted in her seat. 'She's pushing her ship to its very limits to get here as quickly as possible.' I checked my watch. 'They should enter orbit around Dave two hours from now. If your people can be ready to begin loading in about three hours, we'd be grateful.'

'We can do that,' said Elim. 'And what is the plan? How big is the ship? Will it land here?'

I breathed my relief. What a joy it was to work with people who paid attention to details and thought about logistics. 'The *Pequod* is big enough to carry most of your people to the space station. But it doesn't land. It will send a smaller vehicle – a getoff.'

Bexley smoothed her forelock down. 'We'll load the getoff with people and supplies and then send it up to the *Pequod*, where it'll be unloaded. Then it will return and we'll repeat the process. I'm not going to lie to you – this will be hard work. The getoff needs to make two dozen round trips in order to get everyone.'

'If we all work our hardest,' I added, 'we believe it can be done in a bit under two days.'

I expected all the elders to begin signing at once, but for a moment, every hand was still.

Eventually, one of the council members lifted a hand off the desk a few centimetres. This seemed to be a signal that she wished to speak. All heads turned towards her. 'Will we be permitted to bring any property with us?'

I nodded. 'Yes, of course. We've accounted for twenty kilograms per person in our calculations.'

Someone else raised a hand. 'Where will we go?'

It was Bexley who replied this time. 'Well now, that is the question. And the truth is, we don't know. The *Pequod*, the *Teapot*, and a few other ships will transport you to Deep Space Five, a station about six days' journey from here. It's going to be uncomfortable. We'll be jammed in like hay in a bale.'

'It'll be tight,' I acknowledged. 'We'll be uncomfortable and we won't have much of any privacy for those six days. But we'll all be safe and alive.'

'And that station will be our new home?' said the same person again.

'No,' I replied. 'You'll spend the next few months there while you work with the refugee minister and her staff to search for an appropriate home for your people.'

The muscles in Elim's face were tightly clenched. 'And the plenties…?'

I should have seen this question coming. 'They're going to a different station. It's about the same distance – but in a different direction. You'll have light years between yourselves and them.'

'What about our children and our friends – the ones still trapped in Catford?' Elim again.

I nodded. 'We're working on it. Many are already on the

Egg, but we'll ensure that none of them end up going with the plenties unless they choose to do so.'

The room was still.

'Well,' said one of the council members after a moment. 'I guess we'd better get to work.'

———

Progress had continued even in the short time we'd been with the council of elders. Only a handful of tents remained standing. Everywhere I looked, there were neat rolls, bags, and boxes. I found myself wondering how they'd decide what to bring and what to leave behind. Like most species I'd encountered since leaving Earth, the kobolds didn't wear clothes.

What would I take if I could save just twenty kilograms of stuff when I left my home forever? Then I remembered – Spock and I had been kidnapped from Earth with only the clothes I'd been wearing. Well, plus my watch and phone.

'I'm not sure how big the *Pequod*'s getoff is,' said Bexley, jarring me out of my thoughts. 'I mean, I know it can hold eighty-four people. But I don't know how big of a footprint it has. So I suggest we set down over there.' She pointed towards a flat open space, which had probably been part of the city before all the tents came down.

'I'll ask someone to rope off an area for a landing pad,' said Elim.

'Thanks,' I replied. 'People can queue up with their belongings.'

———

Since the kobolds were managing their own evacuation just fine without us, Spock returned to the *Teapot* while Bexley and I headed back to Catford to assist. When I stepped out of my pod, I fought back the urge to scream. There were dozens of plenties visible – and every last one of them was doing something other than boarding a getoff. To our left, a family sat on a picnic blanket, munching on something. Rincy appeared to be arguing with a large group of people – some of whom were holding signs. *More protesters?*

As we headed into the getoff, someone shouted, 'Boycott this chaotic evacuation! We deserve better.' I shook my head and bumped into a couple as they were leaving.

I looked at the taller of the two. 'Where are you going? We're loading the getoff. It needs to depart as soon as it's full. You can't just load your stuff and then go out for dinner.'

Her tail swished in rapid, jerky movements. 'I know that, thank you.'

My hand flapped in a flippant gesture. 'Oh, well at least there's that. Still, we need to load these vehicles and get you up to the *Egg*.'

Her companion had pale greyish-purple fur dotted with lavender. 'Yes, we've just come from there.'

I touched my fingers to my temples, confused. 'You what? What do you mean you just came from there?'

'Was my spouse unclear?' said the first one. She was a sort of tabby – with stripes of varying shades of turquoise. 'We went up to the sky ship to look around and check out the facilities.'

'You what?' I couldn't, I just *couldn't* with these people.

The turquoise hissed. 'You can't expect us to move our entire family up there without first inspecting the accommodations and facilities.'

I gripped one of the seat backs to keep my hands under

control. 'So you went up and what – took a tour? And then you left your belongings unattended and came back down? Is that what you're telling me? Do you have any idea how tight our schedule is? If we cannot get your people off this planet' – my fingers formed tight circles in front of my face – 'you will die. We have less than three days left to evacuate everyone.'

The grey and purple one held up a paw, extending and retracting her claws. 'First of all, no. We did *not* leave our belongings unattended. We look like idiots to you? Our kobold is with them. She's very well-trained.'

Gritting my teeth, I turned and left the getoff. This conversation wasn't going to benefit anyone. Outside, I found Bexley trying to calm Rincy, who was crying.

'Do you see?' wailed Rincy. 'Do you see what I've been putting up with? We can barely get any of them to leave. And the protesters aren't helping matters.' She curled into a ball, pulling her head down to her chest.

Bexley knelt down and stroked her back. 'You're exhausted. When was the last time you took a break?'

Rincy looked up and shook her head. 'I recharged yesterday morning. My battery's down to six per cent.'

'Battery?' I slapped my hands to my mouth – I hadn't meant to say that out loud. *Rincy's a robot! What kind of robot is so disorganised and haphazard?* 'Sorry, I'm sorry. We need to get you back up to your ship so you can ... recharge.'

Bexley stood up and extended a hoof towards Rincy. 'Come on, honey. Let's get you home. Is there a chance your battery will run dry before you plug in?'

Rincy accepted Bexley's proffered arm and pulled herself up into a standing position. 'Not if I leave in the next few minutes. I'll be fine. I should never have let myself run this close to empty. It'll take me at least five hours to charge up.'

Bexley looked me in the eye as she spoke to Rincy. 'Don't you worry, sweetie. I'll take you home. Lem can handle things here for an hour or so, can't you, Lem?'

'Er, yeah. Should be fine. Where are the other people working with you, Rincy?'

Rincy was already waddling towards her pod. 'Aurora's gone into the town centre with a few of the people from the other ships to try to persuade people to evacuate. BB left a few minutes ago.'

I nodded absently. 'Thanks. Slee— Er, recharge well, Rincy. We'll see you later.'

As they left, I walked back to the getoff to see how things were progressing there. Inside, a handful of people dozed in their seats. Returning to the open doorway, I spotted a pure white plenti ambling in my direction, phone in hand. Apple's attention was on the screen and she walked into a tree. I tried to muster some sympathy for her – but the best I could come up with was a general wish that the tree hadn't been harmed.

'Hey, Apple,' I called. 'How's the evacuation going?'

She twisted laconically, looking away from me, her attention never wavering from her screen. Once she'd tapped a few more buttons – with a fully extended claw – she turned to me. 'Bob wants to know why you're not finished yet.'

My eyebrows climbed upwards, threatening to get lost above my hairline. 'I'm sorry? Bob wants to know why we haven't finished saving your species from annihilation yet?'

Apple gave good side-eye – I had to give her that much. I'd never been looked at with so much disdain before – not even by human transphobes. 'Er, yeah. That's what I said, isn't it? Your translator broken or summat?'

I put my hands on my hips, unsure whether I was channelling a petulant child or an exasperated parent. 'No one in Catford has the slightest bit of urgency – least of all Bob. It's all we can do to stop people leaving once they've boarded the getoffs, never mind persuading them to get on in the first place. There's zero accountability from your side. Bob's still sitting in her tastefully appointed office, fiddling with her trinkets and reviewing expense reports while we're out here doing everything possible to stop your people dying. And she has the audacity to—'

'Not even.' Apple's little white nose scrunched up ever so slightly, making her whiskers shiver.

'What?'

'Wha'? Geez, don't eat my head off.' Apple continued to click away on her phone. 'You said Bob was in her office. It ain't even true.'

I plastered a smile I didn't feel onto my face. 'I see. And where is she?'

Apple rubbed herself against the grey bark of the tree she'd bumped into earlier. 'Having lunch wi' t'mayor.'

'What?'

Apple turned back the way she'd come. 'Should really get tha' translator fixed, pet.' She sauntered away.

I sat in the vehicle's open doorway and prodded at the orange grasses encroaching on our territory until Aurora's voice jarred me from my reverie.

'... those bastards!'

I looked up. And then around. Eventually I spotted her. She glowed a mix of transparent and coral, thus rendering her virtually invisible in the orange landscape. 'Hey, Aurora.'

'My apologies,' she added. 'I didn't mean for anyone to overhear my little rant. How much did you catch?'

I grinned tiredly – but more genuinely than I had since leaving Drumheller. 'Nothing really. Only enough to be moderately confident in who you were talking about.'

Henry joined Aurora and me at the evac site in Catford a few minutes later. 'I loaded the kobold language – et voilà!' A hologram image of Henry appeared above her. The virtual Henry extruded two kobold hands and began signing a message.

Aurora shimmered.

I narrowed my eyes. 'What's it, er, what are you saying?'

The real Henry extruded a fan and slapped it at me. 'Well, your AI might have forking interpreted it for you if you hadn't spoken over it, sandwich.'

'Oh.'

I focused on the hologram and Holly began to translate the handspeak into English in Henry's voice.

'… do not have to accompany the plenties. You are being evacuated separately. Report to any of the exodus team for discreet guidance. Attention, kobolds. You do not have to accompany the plenties. You are…'

'Cut the sound on Holo-Henry, please, Holly,' I said. I really hoped the kobolds saw the message, but I'd never be able to hold a conversation – or even think straight – if I had to hear the same instructions over and over again. Turning to Henry, I added, 'That's a great idea. Thanks for thinking of it.'

Aurora shifted to more of a powder blue. 'I second Lem's gratitude, Henry. But I wonder if there's a way we could get the message to more of—'

Henry's absurdly posh voice cut her off. 'I got you covered, gasbag. I've hacked every screen on this bunting planet to show the same info on a loop.'

'*Every* screen?' My mind played Bob's reaction to having her *very important emails* replaced by an image of Henry relaying evacuation messages in koboldian handspeak. It wasn't pretty. 'I'm not sure the plenties are going to like that. In fact, I'm pretty sure they won't.'

'Relax, cheese curd.' Henry spun her wheels on the purple tarmac. 'It's not taking up the whole display. I set it to cover half of each screen. They can look at whatever sparkly toys and laser pointers they like on the other half.'

I spied Apple making her way back across the park towards us. She managed to avoid walking into any trees this time – though that was pure luck rather than because she was looking where she was going. Her eyes were still glued to her screen. She stabbed and swiped at it as she walked. 'Ey up. T' gaffer knows you've done summat to our screens,' she said without looking up. 'She demands you stop immediately.'

I crossed my arms over my chest. 'No.'

That got her attention. 'Wha'd tha say to me?' She reached up a back leg to scratch her ear lazily. 'It's nowt useful besides – just this stupid vacuum cleaner doing some kind of weird dance.'

That took me aback. Could she really not recognise handspeak? I wasn't surprised she didn't understand it – but did she really not even see it was a language? And did she not know that Henry was a person?

'It's … it's not for you,' I stammered. 'You don't need to worry about it. What she's saying doesn't concern you.'

'But *it* doesn't say anything.' Apple's use of the inanimate pronoun pissed me off even more than her ignorance of koboldian handspeak. It was worse even than being misgendered by hateful humans. She wasn't just denying Henry's right to be who she was – she was denying she was anyone at all.

'Go away, Apple.' The job meant I had to save her life; it didn't mean I had to be nice to her.

Apple sat down on the ground. 'Not until you fix the screens. Your little prank isn't even funny. It makes no sense at all.'

Behind Apple, Aurora was now a mix of indigo and pale powder blue. She formed her amorphous cloud-body into an arrow shape drawing my attention away from Apple and Catford. Her vision – however it worked without eyes – was obviously far better than mine. I couldn't see what she was pointing at.

But I trusted her. 'Apple, I swear to frak, if you don't get lost right now, Henry and I will pick you up and strap you into one of the seats in this getoff. We will launch it right this minute – purely for the pleasure of never having to lay eyes on you again. Now piss off!'

Apple hissed at me – but she scarpered. *Thank God for small mercies.*

And then I finally spotted what Aurora had been trying to tell me. There, in the distance, were three kobolds. They were hiding behind a small outbuilding, peering out every few seconds to see if the coast was clear.

'Henry,' I said. 'Are you okay to manage the getoff on

your own for a few minutes while Aurora and I go speak to them?'

There were times when I could *feel* Henry rolling her non-existent eyes at me. 'Oh no. However will I cope with the advancing hordes all on my own? There's an army of plucking cats all fighting one another for a place on the next getoff.' She waved a hinged metal limb haphazardly at all the plenties who *weren't* heading our way.

The best way to deal with her sarcasm was to throw it right back at her. Except nothing came to mind. 'Whatever. We'll be back in a bit. Shout if anyone does show up.'

Aurora was a brilliant royal blue when I looked at her – her version of laughter. 'Shall we see how we can assist our new friends?'

'Yeah, let's go.'

After a couple of metres, Aurora stopped. Patches of magenta grew in her rainbow cloud. 'Oh, hmm.'

I stopped walking and turned to face her. 'What is it?'

'How will we speak with them?' She vibrated slightly as she hovered next to me.

'I can— Oh.' I rubbed my nose. 'Presumably, they understand Persian. But neither of us speaks Persian. We'd be able to understand them, but they wouldn't know what we were saying.'

'Exactly,' she replied.

I put my hands on my hips. 'Huh.'

'I'll go ask Henry to join you,' said Aurora. 'I can take over for her on the getoff.'

'Thanks.' As she returned the way we'd come, I walked towards the kobolds.

One of them – taller than her friends and the most vivid turquoise – walked out from behind the bench.

'Guinan, don't,' signed one of the ones peering out from

behind the safety of park furniture. 'They'll hurt you.' Holly was still running with my alphabetical naming convention.

'We won't hurt you, I promise.' Nodding to the brave one, I added, 'You're very courageous, Guinan. You want to help.'

One of the ones still sort of hiding said, 'I think she's trying to speak to us.'

I spread my arms wide like I'd seen the kobolds in Drumheller do – praying I was right that it meant *yes*.

The three looked at one another suspiciously.

Guinan took a step closer to me. 'Why doesn't she speak?'

Keeping my hands by my side and my voice calm and steady, I said, 'My friend who can sign is on her way. She'll help us talk to one another.' They wouldn't understand me, but I hoped my tone and body language would convey I meant no harm.

I'd grown used to relying on Holly over the past few months. Having to deal with differing languages and forms of communication was suddenly as alien as it had been on Earth.

The four of us were locked in a standoff. I could speak but they wouldn't understand. They could sign – but had no way of knowing if I understood. Instead we all stood perfectly still, studying one another.

After a few moments, Guinan opened her mouth and asked audibly, 'No ... speak ... Persian?'

'My apologies, Lem,' said Holly in its own voice. 'Although she's attempting to communicate, her ability to speak audibly is hindered by her physiology.'

I remembered something. Touching my hand to my chin, I prayed I was right about the sign for *no*.

After a few moments, Henry rolled up alongside me. 'Looks like you needed my help after all, huh, meatsack?' The kobolds all let out startled cries when they saw her.

I kept my eyes on them as I spoke. 'Without translators they have no idea what I'm saying.'

Henry rolled her wheels, turning in a small circle. 'No surprise there. I don't know what you're on about half the time, even with a translator.'

'Ha ha, very funny.' My muscles clenched. 'Can you please do your interpreting thing?'

An appendage that looked like it belonged on a kitchen mixer emerged from Henry's form and sort of whirred at me. 'You mean like in the video?'

I nodded.

'You really are an idiot,' Henry said. 'Honestly, I've never met a dumber muffler parka. What – you think I genuinely grew a pair of koboldian hands for that video?'

I bit my tongue. The kobolds might not understand my words, but they were spooked enough as it was. If I snapped at Henry, they'd bolt. 'Henry, this is life or death. Please. You have nine gazillion different appendages. Surely you've got ones that can approximate hands. Please. Help me out here. No, actually. Don't help me. Do it for them.'

The three kobolds stood, watching us.

'Fine.' A grabby tool with four articulated digits emerged on Henry's left. On her right, she extruded a series of what looked like bendy straws. 'You saw the videos, I take it?'

The three kobolds all held their arms wide – yes.

'My plenti was watching news of the protests this morning,' said a short, rotund one, 'when her screen shifted to show you. She got – well, she swore a lot. And then she spent a lot of time calling her news provider to complain. But I saw. And I understood. I escaped as soon as I could. Can you really help us?'

'We can,' Henry signed. 'If you wait here, we will take

you to Drumheller. From there, you will be evacuated with the rest of your people. Away from the plenties.'

'Drumheller?' asked the third. 'We can go back? But surely we'll be caught.'

'No,' I said. 'You'll leave the plenties behind.'

The kobolds all watched me. Henry's makeshift hands lay still.

I raised my eyebrows at her. 'You know you have to interpret for me, right?'

'You want me to what? Oh, for cat's sake. Brain the size of a —'

'Just do it, Henry.' I lowered my voice. 'Please.'

Henry translated my words for the kobolds.

'But what about the others?' asked Guinan. 'Can anything be done for them?'

'Other kobolds?' asked Henry. 'Can you bring them here in the next hour? We'll bring you with us to Drumheller. But any who miss that flight will meet with your people on the spaceships orbiting the planet. No kobolds will have to go with the plenties.'

The three kobolds faced one another. 'We should take them to free the prisoners,' said the squat one.

Prisoners?

'I'll go with them into town,' said Henry. 'For obvious reasons.'

I touched a finger to my lips. 'If one of them stays with me, I can give her a translator. Maybe she can help interpret for the kobolds that come to the getoff.'

'Not actually a terrible idea, sandwich.' She repeated my suggestion to the kobolds.

Guinan held her arms wide. 'I'll stay.' She took a few hesitant steps towards me.

———

When we got back to the getoff, I rummaged through our supplies until I found a spare translator device. Guinan was wary of me when I motioned for her to put it on, but she did it. It took about fifteen minutes to scan her brain. I tried to reassure her as best I could while we waited, but she sat, watching me with a disappointed look.

Guinan could have spoken to me in that time. My translator worked fine. But she seemed reluctant to do so. I could tell the moment her translator began to work because her eyes opened up like saucers.

I smiled at her. 'Can you understand me now?'

Guinan held her arms wide: Yes. 'You're speaking Persian!'

'You can talk to me. I won't hurt you.' I pointed to the translator on my ear. 'We can talk now.'

She opened her mouth and tried to form words that way. 'We can ... wear ... breakfast?' She was trying to speak Persian – but not clearly enough for Holly.

'My apologies, Lem,' said Holly in its own voice. 'I can't understand her very well. Would it be useful if I showed you images of handspeak?'

I wanted to kick myself for being so stupid. She was hearing my voice in Persian – so she thought I meant she had to speak in Persian too.

'Thanks, Holly,' I said. She didn't need me adding to her worries through my own cack-handed attempts to help. 'Please teach me how to tell her she can use handspeak.'

I pulled out my phone and looked at the screen. I tried to form my hands into the shapes displayed there – but it felt unnatural to my clumsy fingers. But Guinan crept closer and peered at my screen. She looked at me warily.

'You know handspeak?' She signed her words cautiously and slowly.

Her smile was infectious. 'I know it's a language. But really I just wanted you to know that you can sign to me. My translator' – I pointed at my earpiece – 'tells me what you're saying. And now your translator tells you what I'm saying. So we can talk.'

She grinned wide.

'Oh my gosh,' came Bexley's voice from the door of the getoff. 'I got Rincy back to her ship just before her battery crapped out. I had to try to figure out where her charging port was and then carry her – well more like drag her— Oh, hi. You've got a new friend.'

I made the introductions and then we got to work. Guinan helped us organise the few plenties who came. None of them seemed to find it strange that we had a kobold assisting us. In fact, I was horrified by the number of plenties who dumped their bags on her as if she were a porter – or a baggage stand. I did my best to keep her away from those arseholes.

But Guinan was determined to help, so I assigned her to show the incoming kobolds to the outbuilding where I'd first met her. Before long, there were half a dozen kobolds – young and old – hiding behind the shed.

The sound of a ship in atmosphere made me look up. A new and different getoff landed. It set down neatly even though, judging by the vehicle's shape, it was designed for water landings. With its orange-gold exterior it would have stood out nicely in a water landscape – but on this planet, it was hard to see.

Guinan, Bexley, and I ran across the park to the getoff. A panel swung down, becoming a ramp.

'Gracie is requesting to speak with you,' said Holly. 'Shall I put her through or decline the call?'

'Put her through, please.' I glanced to my left to see Bexley was also speaking to her AI.

'Hi, Gracie,' I said. 'Thank you for joining us on such short notice. Is that you in the getoff?'

'I am indeed in the shuttlecraft,' sang Gracie. 'Though for obvious reasons I cannot disembark. I've drained the main body of the vehicle and filled it with an oxygen-nitrogen atmosphere so the aridus species may board.'

'Thanks, Gracie,' said Bexley. 'We really appreciate that. We've got a group of our people wandering the town in search of kobolds – to let them know you'll be evacuating them separately. If you'll give us a minute, I'll call them and —'

'I told you I would arrive at this time,' replied Gracie – her curt words at odds with the sing-songy voice Holly assigned to her. 'It strikes me as incredibly rude of you not to be ready.'

'Gracie,' said Bexley. 'A lot of the kobold population are still being held by the plenties – the mouthspeakers. We've got our people out looking, but it's not been easy.'

'The plenties told them we don't want to evacuate them,' I added. 'They're avoiding us.'

There was a pause and for a moment I wondered if the translator were broken.

'Mouthspeaker arrogance knows no bounds,' she said at length. 'How many survivors have you gathered?'

To be honest, I shared her opinion. 'We have seven kobolds here with us now.'

'Plus there are more on the *Egg*,' added Bexley. 'Almost two hundred, all awaiting transfer to your ship.'

As I was speaking, a large group of kobolds – several

dozen at least – arrived at the site. Some of them looked too sick to be walking. A group of plenties wasn't far behind. Several carried what looked like massive butterfly nets.

'Captain Gracie,' I said. 'Do we have your permission to bring these kobolds into your getoff? I think we need to get them away from here quickly.'

'Damn straight,' she replied. 'But not one plenti is to set foot on my shuttle.'

'Guinan,' I called. 'We need your help, please!'

'Of course. Should I get everyone onto the getoff?'

I was not going to cry right now. I wouldn't let myself. 'Thank you, Guinan. Yes, please. Quick as they can.'

I didn't wait for her reply. In the hour I'd known her, Guinan had shown more diligence and trustworthiness than the entire plenti species.

Bexley and I turned to face the mob. Glancing backwards, I breathed a quick prayer of thanks. The kobolds were safe. All in the getoff. We might have to let them leave without us.

I swallowed down my fear. The angry mob was almost on us.

And who should be leading the pack but Bob. 'What the hell is the meaning of this? Apple messaged me to say you people were going around Catford, kidnapping much-loved pets from people's homes. I said, "No, never." I defended you, you ungrateful bastards. How dare you steal from us. I said to her – I said, "They may be lazy and incompetent and, sure, maybe they're unaccountably behind on this disastrously disorganised evacuation project. But they wouldn't *steal* from us." And yet here you are, making a liar of me. I demand an explanation!'

The horde behind her heaved angrily. They were out for

blood. And there were only two of us. But the kobolds rushed to our aid, fighting back against their oppressors.

'They're people, Bob,' I shouted. 'They have the same rights as you do. We're evacuating them separately.'

My words were swallowed up by the roar of the angry crowd. We were pushed back as far as the doorway. Bexley brayed for Gracie to close the door and take off.

The ramp lifted into the air, knocking me off my feet. I nearly fell out as we flew – but three kobolds gripped me in strong hands. The fall wouldn't have killed me – we were only a metre off the ground. But Bob and her angry mob of hench-cats might have.

I breathed a sigh of relief as the ramp-door swung shut with Bexley, me, and three dozen kobolds flying away to safety.

Ten minutes later we touched down at the Drumheller evac site. When the ramp-door swung down this time, I was in for another shock. The good kind this time.

The entire city had been dismantled in the three hours since we'd left. The kobolds sat in an orderly queue, each with their belongings.

When Bexley and I stepped out of the ship, Dinah ran to greet us, sporting a bright white bow around her neck.

I stood there gawping like an idiot. 'Dinah, this is bloody brilliant. How did you – everyone, I mean – get so much done in so little time?' I couldn't stop grinning.

Bexley knelt down and hugged Dinah. 'You did good.'

Dinah hugged her back then leaned away so she could sign. 'Everyone helped. Even the littles. And we fitted a dozen Persian-understanders with translators. So they can translate for you. They're wearing white bows. You should be able to spot an interpreter even from a distance.'

Bexley reached out a hoof and touched Dinah's necker-chief. 'Clever! What a great idea.'

Dinah made a serious face. 'Fenchurch is gone, though.

She took her family and a couple dozen others and set off for the caves.'

I grimaced. That was disappointing – but not all that surprising. 'I'm sorry.'

Dinah took a deep breath before spreading her arms wide and then touching her chin. 'It was their choice. Is the ship ready for us to load? We don't have all year, you know.'

I grinned. 'It is – but we've got thirty-six people on board already. This vehicle is larger than the ones we're using in Catford, so there's room for another forty-eight people with their stuff.'

'Then let's get moving.' She pulled a whistle out from under her scarf and blew three quick, shrill tones. People began filing into the ship in an orderly fashion.

'Oh my gosh,' exclaimed Bexley. 'You're going to have this done in no time.'

———

Eight hours later, I was absolutely exhausted. Two of the *Teapot*'s blue pods landed not far away from the getoff. Bexley and I headed over to say hello.

When the door of the first blue phone box opened, BB stepped out. 'Hello, you two. I brought you some dinner.' She held three sealed plastic containers up. 'And I thought Spock would appreciate the chance to stretch her legs for a bit before bed.'

'Thanks, BB. I'm sure you're right.' I headed over to the second pod to free my dog.

When I pulled open the door to her pod, she practically jumped into my arms. 'Lem! Lem! Lem! Spock missed Lem!'

As usual, a crowd of kobold children gathered around us as soon as Spock made an appearance. They all wanted to pet her at once. She wouldn't hurt them – but I still kept a close eye on everything.

'Thanks for dinner, BB,' said Bexley. 'It's great that the kobolds want to share their food with us. I loved the dishes they served us. Absolutely delicious. But I can't eat very much – it's a bit spicy for my tastes.' She could say that again. I still had blisters from our previous meal. 'So… What'd you bring me?'

BB clucked. 'I brought you mushy peas – I hope that's okay.'

Bexley had had mushy peas before – or whatever dish it was that Holly translated that way. It didn't smell anything like peas to me. And of course, it looked like the same drab nutrient porridge it actually was.

'And, Lem,' BB continued. 'I wasn't sure what you wanted to eat so I took a guess. You're always talking about how much you miss coffee – so I flavoured yours like that.'

Weird, but okay. 'Thanks, BB. I appreciate it.'

'And I know how Spock likes to have company when she eats, so I brought her food with me as well.'

I watched as three new kobold children took the place of the last four – giving Spock all the fuss and attention she wanted. 'Thanks. Vindaloo, I assume?'

'No, she requested something called macaroni cheese this evening,' said BB.

Spock almost knocked one of the kids over as she ran to BB. 'Feed Spock?'

I apologised to the kids and checked that everyone was okay. Then we headed to the break area beside the loading zone. BB took over for us.

Once I'd dropped to the ground, I pulled the lid off one of the dishes. Spock immediately tried to stick her head in as the scent of coffee filled the air.

I took the dish away from her. 'Excuse me! I think you'll find this one's mine. Now sit on your bum and wait like a good girl.'

She did so, her tongue hanging out and her tail swishing. 'Feed Spock, please.'

I pulled the lid off the other container – the smell made my mouth water. When I'd set the bowl down for her, I picked up my coffee-flavoured gloop and tucked in.

'Not a bad day's work, eh?' said Bexley after a few minutes. Fifty metres away, the getoff was pulling up its ramp-door and getting ready to launch.

I nodded. 'More than five hundred people now. It's amazing! And no one's whinging about the accommodations.'

Bexley tapped her hooves on the ground in front of herself. 'Nobody loads their belongings onto the getoff and then wanders off in search of a restaurant. It's nice not having to field endless complaints about the lack of snacks and in-flight entertainment on the eighteen-minute flight to the *Pequod*.'

I heaved a contented sigh. 'Best of all? No Apple. And no Bob.'

Bexley nickered. 'Amen to that.' After a moment, she added, 'You going right to sleep when you get back to the *Teapot*?'

I'd been working for thirteen straight hours – I was exhausted. I waved my phone in the air. 'Got some messages to listen to first.' I checked the screen for the updated numbers. 'Thirty-eight missed calls from Apple and six more from Bob herself. After the first eight, I told Holly to decline all future calls from them automatically.'

'Good th—' But that was as far as Bexley got because Bob's voice burst through my earpiece, drowning Bexley out and making me jump.

'This time you're going to listen to me, Lem. I have had it up to here with your insolence. You're taking risks with our lives. You may think this is a funny game – but I don't know what you're playing at. Abandoning my people in the middle of a job we're paying you for in order to go play in the wilderness with a bunch of animals—'

'Holly, can you shut her up, please?'

'I'm sorry, Lem,' said Holly – layered over Bob's continued rantings. 'I'm afraid I can't do that – I'm locked out of my own controls.'

'And don't even think about trying to hang up on me,' Bob roared. 'I've taken the liberty of removing your ability to disconnect or mute this call. You're going to listen to me. As you know, the galactic prime minister is a close, personal friend of mine. I'll have you brought up on charges of genocide, terrorism, and dereliction of duty. Your actions since arriving on planet Dave amount to high treason. You will—'

I heaved an earth-shattering sigh as Bob's histrionics were finally cut off.

Bexley waved her hooves in my face. 'I asked Henry to cut the call off,' she shouted into the now silent air.

'Yeah, I know,' I bellowed back – before realising what I was doing and dropping my voice. 'Yeah, she succeeded. Holy potato, that was awful.' I pinched the bridge of my nose. 'I don't have to worry, do I? She said she was going to have me charged with genocide and terrorism.' The weight of the last few days suddenly felt like it was pressing on my shoulders. A noise that was partway between a sigh and a sob escaped my lips. 'Can she do that?'

I couldn't stop my lips trembling – and the rest of my body followed. Collapsing to the ground, I broke down in tears.

Bexley sat next to me and held me while I cried. 'You

haven't done anything wrong and we can prove it. And I don't believe the minister is her friend. Any minister. Not for one second.'

Spock ran over and joined us. 'Be okay, Lem.' She licked my face and sat down on my feet.

I cried for a few minutes – until the wracking sobs slowed. Bexley pulled an enormous hankie from her holster and passed it to me. I wiped my face and blew my nose.

Taking a slow calming breath I counted primes in my head. *Two, three, five, seven, eleven, thirteen, seventeen, nineteen, twenty-three, twenty-nine.* 'Sorry, I'm sorry. I just need a minute.'

'You should go back up to the *Teapot*,' said Bexley. 'Get some rest.'

I considered it as I rubbed Spock's chest. *Inhale. Hold. Thirty-one, thirty-three, thirty-seven, forty-one. Exhale.* 'All right. Shall we go home for a bit, Spock?'

Spock twirled in circles. 'Home!'

I looked up at Bexley. 'You sure you're all right to keep going?'

She extended a hoof to help pull me up off the ground. 'Absolutely, I'm good. You go. BB and I will keep things moving along here. Aurora said she'd join us in a bit too. We'll be fine. When we need to rest, Aurora and Henry can take over. Or you'll be back. We'll make it work.'

I nodded slowly. 'Right. Thanks. Oh and, hey?'

She tilted her head. 'Yeah?'

'Can you thank Henry for me, please? If she hadn't intervened once again, I'd still be stuck listening to Bob scream.'

Bexley smiled as we walked over to where the pods were. 'You know what to do if it happens again, right?'

I looked up at her, the weariness making the planet's light gravity seem heavy. 'What's that?'

'Just take your earpiece out.'

I chuckled. No idea why that hadn't occurred to me before.

————

Holly was singing Lady Gaga's 'Poker Face' at me. Its voice was flat and off key.

I rolled out of bed and went through the motions of getting ready. I spat my toothpaste out and glared at my reflection. 'When this is over, we're going to sleep for a week.' My reflection didn't reply.

'Holly,' I said. 'What time is it?'

'By shipboard time, it is six minutes after midnight.'

My days and nights were all out of whack. I'd been working fifteen-hour days followed by about six hours of sleep – which meant I woke up each day a few hours earlier than the day before.

My room was a mess. I grabbed a pile of laundry and tossed it into the bag next to my desk. 'Ugh. I'm going to have to clean this place up at some point in the next day or two.' We'd be overrun with kobolds on the trip to Deep Space Five. The Teapotters had agreed to share Ten Backwards. Our rooms would each accommodate several families of kobolds.

'Come on, Spock,' I said. 'Let's go get some breakfast.'

That woke her up. She jumped down off the bed and wagged her tail. 'Feed Spock?'

As we walked towards the lift, I asked Holly if there was anyone else on the ship.

'BB has just returned to the *Teapot*. She is in the kitchen. Shall I ring her for you?'

'Nah, I'll be there in a minute anyway. Cheers.'

The lift carried us down to the ship's lowest level. When the doors slid open, I was greeted by the sound of ... music? Spock ran off ahead of me.

It sounded live – not recorded. As if someone was singing – just not in a style I recognised. I didn't think there were any musical instruments in play, but with alien voices it could be hard to tell what was a voice and what wasn't. This sounded a bit like a classically trained opera singer trying to recreate the sound of clanging spoons.

'I've been hearing spangles.' With Holly translating, it morphed into BB's voice. Only singing. 'Feels like a technicolour – technicolour. Everyone is pink sometimes. You're looking like the bling love. And you must think that I'm twinkling. So stop your glimmering. Because I found the glow for me.'

I stopped moving – didn't want to embarrass BB. But the spell was broken when she squawked a moment later.

'Oh, Spock! My goodness, you scared the life out of me,' said BB. 'Good evening or good morning or whatever time of day it is to you.'

I rushed down the corridor to catch up with Spock. Ducking into the kitchen, I said, 'Morning, BB. Everything all right?'

BB lifted her wings in greeting. 'Yes, yes. I was just startled when Spock walked in on me while I was ... I hope I didn't disturb you.' Her cheeks – bare of feathers – flushed bright pink.

Hoping to stop my own blush, I pinched my lips together for a moment. 'I ... er ... I thought I could hear someone singing. It was beautiful.'

She turned away. 'Oh gosh. I'm so sorry. It's our song – Aurora's and mine. I didn't mean for... That is, I didn't know...' She opened a cupboard and stared at the contents.

As I prepared Spock's breakfast, I decided to give BB a break. 'Did you just get back from Drumheller?'

Little hands emerged from under her wings and crossed over her waist protectively. 'Yes, I returned a few minutes before … a few minutes ago.'

Once I set Spock's breakfast down, I returned to the food dispenser. I tapped in the code for porridge with peanut butter, bananas, and a dash of maple syrup. Not that it had any oats, peanuts, fruit, or maple – but it would taste like all those things. 'How's the evacuation going?' The machine calculated my nutrient requirements and then paired them with the relevant chemicals to give it the flavours I requested. It spat out a coarse pale pink powder.

BB briefly raised and lowered her crest partway – her equivalent of a shrug. 'I don't know how they're managing it – but they're ahead of schedule. You set a pretty tight timetable. I was sceptical about whether it was achievable. Especially after working in Catford. But they're actually about half an hour ahead of time.'

The dispenser added a stream of steaming hot water to my bowl of powder. I picked it up and stirred it. The pink powder lost its colour on contact with the water, going a sort of beige grey. 'That's incredible. Honestly, the kobolds are a joy to work with. I absolutely hate the thought of anyone taking advantage of them.'

BB removed a mug from the cupboard and walked to the food dispenser. With her back to me, she tapped buttons with her talons. 'I detest oppression and abuse. Slavery is —'

The sharp sound of breaking ceramic pierced the air – followed swiftly by the tinkling of shards of her mug landing on the hard floor.

When she turned to face me, blood was flowing freely from the centre of one of her stiffened hands. It was only then I recalled that Aurora had been enslaved by the bunny-boos for almost four years. It had torn their lives apart.

Swiping a towel from the sink, I ran to BB. She pressed the fabric into her hand. 'Oh dear. I'm afraid I'm finding this mission more stressful than I'd like to admit.'

I held her taloned hand as she pressed the fabric to the wound. 'I'm sorry. This must bring back terrible memories. I can't imagine what it must have been like for you – or for Aurora.'

BB had gone to desperate lengths to get her spouse back. Including kidnapping a number of unsuspecting people to help with her plan.

BB fluffed her feathers indignantly. 'I was fine. I'm not the one who was in captivity – held against my will. It wasn't me who was unable to leave the ship or communicate with anyone. I'm not the one who was called *it*. Do you have any idea how demeaning it is when someone uses the inanimate pronoun – as if you weren't actually a person.'

People stubbornly refusing to call you by the right pronoun? Now, that I did know about. Being misgendered hurt. A lot. Never being sure if I was going to get beat up for using the toilet or called a pervert or a misogynist just for daring to exist in public.

'Aurora doesn't like to show her trauma. But did you know she dreams of them? I didn't want us to remain on the *Teapot* after what happened to her here. I don't like to be reminded. But she wants to build happy memories here. She views our time here as a reclamation of her ... an assertion of ... I don't know. But I love her. And I'll do whatever it takes to make her happy and to help her rebuild her life.'

She clutched the towel to her injured hand and bent down to pluck some of her feathers with her beak. 'I'm sorry. It's unfair of me to unload all this on you. And I really shouldn't have told you all that about Aurora. This mission is bringing up painful memories.' She waved her injured hand around. 'I'm not coping very well.'

Putting my arm around her shoulders, I steered her towards the door. 'Come on, BB. Let's go to the medlab.'

She ground her beak. 'I'm sorry you had to witness that.' She peeled the bloodied fabric back from her hand – sending more blood spurting into the air. 'Annoyingly, I'd be grateful for your assistance to get this stitched up if that's okay. I can talk you through the procedure.'

Pinching my lips together, I breathed in through my nose. I was such a wimp – I couldn't even clip Spock's nails myself. Sewing someone's skin together was going to stretch me to my limits. But BB needed me so I'd do my best.

———

Once we got BB's hand sorted and cleaned up the mess, she went to bed and I sat down to work on the logistics – planning for who would travel in each ship. Gracie had handed over getoff-piloting responsibilities to one of her team for a few hours, so she and I got together with Rincy – through the magic of technology – to hammer out a plan that caused the least inconvenience to all involved.

'Frankly,' sang Gracie, 'I don't give a toss how much the plenties endure. They should all be crowded together in a single cell and hauled straight to the courthouse on Trantor.' Her flipper-legs danced rapidly around her as she sang – then slowed right down. 'But I suppose the crews of the other ships should not suffer for saving their lives. As such, the disruption must be shared equally amongst all.'

Rincy's cluttered, chaotic office butted up against Gracie's pool and my seat on the *Teapot*. 'Er, yes,' said Rincy. 'That's an excellent point. And, while I think we all share a similarly low opinion of the plenties, our views are irrelevant. We've been hired to evacuate the planet – not to pass judgement on the residents of Dave.'

Gracie harrumphed. 'I will opine on anyone I choose.'

I ground my teeth to stifle a yawn. 'How are things going on Catford? How many people still need to be evacuated?'

Rincy picked up a tablet, looked at it, clicked a few buttons – then tossed it aside. She picked up a different one and repeated the process. 'I've just had an update. As of a few minutes ago, we've evacuated almost twenty-four hundred people – mostly plenties, obviously, but several hundred kobolds as well.'

Gracie waved her tail. 'Yes, two hundred and fourteen kobolds have transferred aboard the *Pequod* from the *Egg* so far. We will welcome as many kobolds as we can fit – around sixteen hundred. It won't be comfortable, but it's feasible.'

I nodded. 'Thank you, Gracie. We appreciate your efforts on the kobolds' behalf. The *Teapot* can accommodate about a hundred kobolds. And likewise, it will be … cosy. But we can manage for a few days.'

Rincy propped herself up on the arm growing out of her chest – a sort of one-handed push-up. 'Between the two sites, we're looking at around twenty-three hundred kobolds. Your two ships can take the majority of that, so I need to free up ships that will accommodate another six hundred. Which means the plenties are also going to be crammed in' – she waved a hand, sending a pile of junk flying – 'tighter than they like. Bob is not going to be happy about this.'

'Bob is lucky I don't lock her in my fridge,' roared Gracie. Instinctively, I ducked out of the way of the wall of holo-graphic water she sent my way – though of course, it faded from view at the edge of her display.

Rincy raised a webbed hand. 'Believe me, I know. You won't get any disagreement from me.'

Bexley arrived back on the *Teapot* for her rest break as the meeting wrapped up. Spock and I headed down to the transporter room to meet her.

She woke up and did her post-transport zoomies, then said, 'Oh my gosh, what a fun day this has been. We just launched our fourteenth getoff. Almost twelve hundred kobolds already. Can you believe it? Everything is so neat and organised and – okay, so we've had a few squabbles over who's travelling with whom and who gets to bring what and there was a set of divorced parents who all refused to travel on the same ship together but who also refused to let their shared child travel on a different ship from them —'

She blew a noisy breath out.

I smiled at my friend. 'It's going well?'

'Amazing,' she said. 'Anyways, I'm famished. Let's get some dinner, shall we?' She turned and bolted out of the room.

I followed her. 'So, I take it we're still on track to get everyone off-world by midnight?' I ducked through the door into the kitchen.

Bexley tapped buttons on the food dispenser. 'Pretty sure we're going to be done ahead of schedule, actually.' When the machine added the boiling water, the scent of freshly mown grass filled the room.

She removed her bowl and I took my turn at the dispenser. As always, when faced with the choice of what to eat, I struggled to think of what I wanted. The best way to avoid an indecision loop was to tap in the first thing that popped into my head. In this case, that was peanut butter ice cream. *Hey, if you could have a nutritionally balanced lunch that tasted like peanut butter ice cream, wouldn't you?*

Holly sang me awake on the whatevereth day since our arrival at planet Dave with a vigorous but tuneless rendition of Toto's 'Africa'.

The first thing I asked was, 'How close are we to completing the evacuation of Drumheller?'

Holly stopped singing mid-sentence. 'The last getoff docked with the *Pequod* fifty-four minutes ago.'

My arms fell slack at my sides, startling Spock. 'They did it,' I whispered. I swung my legs over the edge of the bed. 'They did it.' As relief flooded my body, I got up and danced around the room. 'They did it,' I sang over and over.

I stopped dancing mid-whirl. 'Holly, how many people are still in Catford?'

'Rincy's latest report indicates there are still five hundred and forty-four residents plus sixteen members of the exodus team.'

I dropped back onto the bed, fatigue coursing through my blood like a pathogen. 'Bollocks.' I let out a long slow breath, continuing until my lungs burnt with the effort.

Eleven hours until impact and there were still so many people to evacuate!

———

When we arrived in the kitchen a few minutes later, Aurora already had our breakfast ready to go.

'Hello, tickle friend! Feed Spock?'

Aurora responded by passing an appendage through Spock's face. 'Good morning, my dears. Did you sleep well?'

It didn't seem to matter how many times I told her she didn't have to make my meals or clean up after me. 'I did, thanks. Holly says the Drumheller evacuation is complete – more than an hour ahead of schedule.'

Aurora did ... whatever it was she did to make her tray float, guiding it into the mess. 'Indeed. I spoke with Gracie a few minutes ago. She's going to start ferrying kobolds to the other ships shortly. We're due to receive our first group an hour from now.'

I lifted one of the bowls from the tray and peeled off the lid. The delicious aroma of sweet potato vindaloo filled my nose. I set that bowl down on the floor for Spock – and then lifted the lid off the other. Aurora always chose flavours for my meals based on the data in my preferences – but she didn't always understand the nuances of human tastes. I'd once had a meal flavoured entirely like garlic. And another one that combined pizza, brownies, and beer – all in a single bowl of nutrient porridge. But I was lucky this time: baked beans.

Aurora floated into the centre of the room. 'Will you be going to Catford after breakfast?'

'Uff. Uh fpove—' I swallowed my mouthful of sweet, smoky, spicy porridge. 'Sorry. I suppose I'd better. There's still almost six hundred people to evacuate. Rincy needs all the help she can get.'

'I cannot wait for this job to be done.' Aurora wafted through my hair, ruffling it as she drifted back towards the kitchen. 'Stay safe.'

———

Half an hour later, I climbed out of my pod at the Catford evac site.

Bexley galloped over and flung her arms around me. 'Lem, oh my gosh. Drumheller has been safely evacuated. Everyone's safely on the *Pequod* now. Oh, duh! You must already know that – or else you wouldn't be here. Anyways, how'd you sleep? Are you ready for another day of ... you know ... arguing with plenties?'

I sucked in a deep breath. 'Yeah, I spent the trip down here psyching myself up. Well, in between all the screaming.'

She rubbed my arm as she guided me across the park. 'Come on, I'll show you what we've been doing. We're going around to all the houses. If we find anyone still home, we pretty much drag them down to the evacuation centre.' She glanced up at me, her brows knit tightly together. 'Not literally, though. Consent still matters. Obviously.'

At the first house, we found a family watching television. In the third house, no one appeared to have packed anything. The seventh door we knocked on was answered by an elderly plenti who hissed at us and said the asteroid was 'a liberal plot to rid the planet of undesirables' like her.

She was still lecturing us on the disrespect of today's youth when I spied a familiar white plenti out the corner of my eye.

'Ey up, Lem,' called Apple – without looking up from her

phone. 'I warned you, I did. Bob's proper radged wi' you. She says you're to see her in her office straight away.'

The person whose house we were standing in front of continued railing against the plot to rid Catford of the old and gullible. Turning away from her, I said to Apple, 'I'm not going to Bob's office.'

Bexley abandoned the vitriol-spewing plenti and charged up to Apple. 'We're trying to get everyone off this planet before the asteroid hits. Which in case you've forgotten is about nine hours from now. If it wasn't the day season, it would dominate the sky by this point. We can see it from the ships and, let me tell you, I don't want to be on this planet when it strikes. Anyone who's still here will die, Apple. So if you don't mind, we've got more important things to do than listen to Bob's latest tirade about the way the evacuation is being run.'

I felt a tugging on my sleeve. When I looked at the elderly plenti in the doorway, she looked terrified. Just a frightened pensioner. 'Is it true?'

The rage in my head gave way to a sort of dull annoyance. And then to pity. Yes, this person had ignored the warnings. Not just ignored them – she'd advised others not to listen to them. But she was still a person. A scared, helpless person.

I pinched the bridge of my nose. 'Yes. And we only have a few hours. We need to evacuate you before the asteroid strikes. There's room for everyone, but you have to leave *now*.'

She turned to face the inside of her house. For a second I thought she was taking one last look around, but then she bellowed. 'Helo! Get my meds and my walking stick. We're leaving. Helo? You hear me?' Looking back at me, she added, 'Sorry, you'll have to forgive Helo – she's an idiot.'

Behind her, a form appeared. It was the smallest and skinniest kobold I'd seen yet. She had orange bruises on her face and in a trail along her shoulder and down one arm.

'Bexley,' I whispered. I didn't want to turn around – so I waved my hand trying to get her attention.

'I know.' Bexley took my hand. 'I see her.'

The plenti reached out to support herself on the door. 'Well, come on. We haven't got all day … apparently.'

I looked at her, my jaw hanging slack – still seeing her as the helpless pensioner I'd discovered only a moment ago but now seeing her for the vicious abuser she also was. 'Sorry, what?'

Her tail swished back and forth slowly. 'Give me your arm, dumbass. I need help getting through the doorway.' Of course – the portal-door was about half a metre off the ground.

Silently, I held out my arm. She took it in hers – claws retracted, thankfully – and braced herself against me as she hauled herself out. 'You'll need to lift Helo out. Stupid thing's too small to climb out on her own – which is both a blessing and a curse.' She looked back into the house. 'Helo, get your ungrateful arse to this door right now. We're leaving.'

Helo looked like she was going to flee.

'It's okay,' I said. 'I won't hurt you, I promise. We'll take you somewhere safe.'

But, of course, Helo had no translator. She understood Persian – but I was speaking English. She looked at me with sheer terror in her eyes – and took a step backwards.

'Don't make me come back in there,' shrieked the elderly plenti.

But then I felt a new touch on my elbow. 'It's okay, Lem. I've got this.'

I looked down. 'Dinah? What are you doing in Catford? It isn't safe. You shouldn't be here.'

She smiled up at me and climbed over the threshold.

'Hey, get that animal out of my house,' screeched the elderly plenti.

'It's okay.' And unexpected calm washed over me. 'Dinah will help lift Helo out. We'll collect your meds and your stuff and we'll take you to the getoff. You'll be safe.' *And Dinah will get Helo away from you.*

As we headed out, I looked back over my shoulder to check. Sure enough, Dinah had the child in her arms. Once they were over the doorway, Dinah sprinted away with the child clutched tightly to herself. Bexley and I supported the old plenti all the way to the ships.

It wasn't until we were helping her get strapped into her seat that she called out for Helo again. When we left the getoff, she was still hurling invective and abuse at a child who was thankfully too far away to hear.

'Well,' I said when we were safely out of earshot. But then I had no idea where to take that sentence.

Bexley tapped her hooves in the air in front of herself. 'Yeah, tell me about it.'

We stopped for a breather under the shade of a tall coral-coloured tree. I slumped down on my arse and pulled my thermos of helbru from my bag. 'How did Dinah show up at exactly the right moment?' I raised the purple stimulant to my lips then changed my mind, opting for the flask of plain water instead.

'I called her. Soon as I heard that plenti shouting at someone in the house, I figured it would be a kobold.' Bexley swallowed then wiped her face with her arm.

I screwed the lid back on the water bottle and put it in my bag. 'Wasn't she on the *Pequod*? How'd she get here so fast?'

Bexley took a bite of her protein bar and chewed it. 'No, she and a group of about a dozen kobolds came back to help search Catford for more of their people to be evacuated.'

'Wow.' I leaned back against the tree.

'Did you see the bruises on that kid – Helo?'

'What the hell have we got ourselves into here?' I let my head fall to my knees.

'I know.' Bexley leaned against me. 'It really sucks.'

I gulped down as much air as I could hold in my lungs. 'We're here to save lives – and that's what we're doing.'

Bexley touch-tapped her hooves on the orange grass. 'And we saved that plenti just now. She may be a horrible person, but she's alive because of us.'

'Yeah, I suppose.' I sat up and wiped tears from my eyes with my sleeve. 'As long as she draws breath there's still a chance she'll change. It's never too late for second chances.'

'Helo will be checked out by one of the kobold doctors,' said Bexley. 'Her injuries will be documented. That plenti will be charged with abuse. If she's found guilty then she'll be rehabilitated and re-educated. And Helo will be safely out of her reach forever.'

I stood and offered a hand to help Bexley up.

'It's a start.' She blew out a noisy breath and accepted my hand.

A pod was just setting down – blue, so I knew it was one of ours. We wandered over, arriving at the landing site just as Henry exited the pod.

'Hey, Henry,' I said. 'Cheers for joining us.'

Henry wheeled over to where Bexley and I stood. 'Never let it be said I don't earn my frolicking pay packet.'

Bexley pushed her too-short mane behind her shoulders. 'There's still another quarter of the town to search. May as well get back at it.'

Dinah joined us as we started down the street together.

Once Bexley was finished hugging her, I nodded at Dinah in greeting. 'Thanks for your help. Did you get Helo settled safely?'

Dinah smiled sadly, her arms wide. 'Yeah, one of our doctors is looking after her.'

'Rincy and I mapped out the town and divided it up into sections for us to go door-knocking on the last day,' said Bexley. 'I've got the list that we're supposed to cover. It'll take us about ten minutes to get there.' As we walked, one of the getoffs launched. 'Rincy's trying to get everyone off in another four hours. I don't know if it's doable, but we don't have that much longer.'

'Plucking asteroid is almost here,' said Henry.

We reached the first house and pressed the doorbell. But before anyone could answer – if anyone was even home – something hit me and I died.

Okay, so I wasn't dead – but I was cold and uncomfortable. I wasn't sure how long I'd been asleep, but I didn't feel refreshed. And why was I sitting upright? My face was pressed against a hard surface and I'd been drooling on my chest.

Bending my head down, I rubbed my eyes on my shoulder and looked around. Cold oxygen blew up my nose. Nothing was quite in focus, though. I cringed at an irritation in my arm.

'This doesn't feel like home,' I muttered to myself. 'It's not the *Teapot*. Where's Spock? Why do I have such a headache? And what's that infernal bleeping?'

Then I remembered … something. We'd been on the planet Dave, trying to evacuate the local population. Something was poking my arm.

A bleeping noise drew my attention. I blinked my eyes rapidly, trying to bring things into focus.

Bob's office? Why was I in Bob's office? 'Bob?'

It dawned on me that my hands were tied behind my back. To something. I couldn't move.

The bleeping and poking persisted. I looked over my shoulder. 'Henry! Thank God you're here. What's happening?'

Henry bleeped some more. And then jabbed me in the face with … I don't know … maybe a spoon.

'Why are we in Bob's office?'

Instead of answering me, Henry emitted a string of annoyed-sounding bleeps. And stabbed me again. In the arm this time. With what looked like a toothbrush.

'Stop poking me, you freak,' I said. I wanted to swat her appendages away. But, you know, tied up. 'Tell me what's going on.'

Henry wheeled backwards by about half a metre and extruded a familiar-looking implement. When had I seen that one before? She pulled the two blades apart and snipped them viciously.

'Scissors! Those are the scissors you used to chop Bexley's hair. Why are you snapping scissors at me, you bastard?' I leant away from her. Then a thought struck me. 'Hey, you couldn't untie me, could you?'

Henry extruded a dozen or more appendages of differing shapes and sizes. And every last one of them flopped indignantly. Once she'd retracted the rest, she snipped the scissors again. Menacingly.

I turned my body as far as I could away from her, so she could access the ties fixing my hands in place.

Aside from the tugging sensation and the sound of Henry cutting my ties, everything was strangely still. At least they'd left me with my oxygen mask.

I rubbed my wrists together to try to get the circulation back. 'Cheers, Henry.' I pulled myself to my feet and looked out the window. 'Something's taken a little bite out of the sun.' I turned to face Henry.

A long thin object swung down from Henry and snapped open like a hand fan. Then she slapped herself with it.

'Yeah, yeah, all right. I'm an idiot. I get it. Aren't you going to call me names? Maybe insult my parentage?' I rubbed my neck. 'Hey, why aren't you talking? Usually there's no shutting you up.'

She bleeped at me.

'For real?'

Again with the bleeping.

'Did you lose your voice? When they ... whatever ... kidnapped us, did they do something to your voice?'

Henry did her magic eyeless glare.

'Whatever. I'll enjoy not having to listen to you for a bit. Hey, Holly?'

No response. And I finally – finally – looked at my watch, where Holly 'lived'. Only it wasn't there. I touched my ear – no earpiece either.

'Bollocks.' I wobbled as I jabbed my fists into my sides. 'Well, I guess we'd better get back to the evacuation site.'

Henry bleeped at me again as I walked to the door.

I heaved the crank handle to open it, still fighting the fogginess in my brain. 'Come on. Let's ... oh.'

Henry emitted a long, thin stream of bleeps.

'I suppose I can ... er, that is, if you don't mind ... I could lift you over the portal.'

She slapped herself with the fan again.

'Well, do you want to get out of here or not?'

She extruded two articulated metal 'arms' and sort of shrugged.

'Come on then,' I said. 'It's got to be worth a shot, right?'

Begrudgingly, she rolled forwards.

I raised my hands and tried to figure out the best way to grip her smooth, cylindrical shape. 'Er, may I?'

Two solid-looking handles appeared – one on either side of her.

'Thanks.'

Bleep.

I gripped them and heaved. She lifted maybe a centimetre or two off the ground. Nowhere near the half metre we needed. 'Frak me, Henry. What the hell are you filled with?' Even in this planet's low gravity, there was no way I could lift her high enough to get her over the lip of the portal.

Angry bleeping. The handles retracted into her body and a new one appeared atop her flat lid.

I stared down at her. 'What the hell is that for? I can't lift with two handles. What makes you think I can lift you with one?'

She rolled up to the door and extruded a ... it looked a bit like a leg. Sort of. She propped it up against the wall.

I looked at her blankly.

A shrill, steady bleep sounded.

'What?'

A second appendage oozed out of her and swung towards me. It mimed a lifting motion. I lined myself up parallel with her and tried to mimic her movements – bracing my leg against the wall and lifting.

A puff of air was released from a hidden vent somewhere on Henry's body.

'What?'

With her newest 'arm' she tapped the wall under the doorway. Then she raised it up and pointed towards the opening above.

'Okay, I think I get you. Hang on.' I climbed through the open portal. When I had braced myself against the wall, I leant in and grabbed Henry's handle again. I grunted with the effort, hoisting Henry a good ten centimetres off the floor – before dropping her unceremoniously.

She toppled onto her side and rolled across the floor, emitting a loud, discordant string of bleeps. I had no doubt that Holly would have translated them as a series of short guttural words.

I felt a gentle prodding on my right hip. 'Dinah! Where did you come from? Are you okay?'

Her hands were tied behind her back like mine had been. She made a series of mouth-noises – not that I understood any of them.

'Henry,' I called. 'Dinah's here. Hopefully, between us we can lift you over – but first we need you to cut her free.'

Bleep.

Dinah clambered over the portal edge and I followed her back into Bob's office. Together, we hefted Henry back into a standing position and then she cut Dinah's bonds.

'Right,' I said. 'Henry, you can understand me, right?'

Bleep bleep.

'Okay, I assume that means yes. But can we make a simple system where one bleep means yes and two mean no?'

Henry seethed for a moment – at least I imagine that's what she was doing. Bleep. She extruded the same two *arms* she'd used last time we needed her to sign and began talking to Dinah.

'Excellent. That's a start.' I took a deep breath. 'Henry, can you ask Dinah if she's okay, please?'

Bleep.

'Is that yes, you asked already and she's fine or yes, you can ask her?'

Bleep.

'Right, sorry.' I scratched my head. This was harder than I expected. 'Have you already asked her if she's okay?'

Bleep.

Quick deep breath. 'And she is?'

Bleep.

'That's good.' I turned to Dinah. 'I'm glad. Henry, can you tell her what we discussed, please? And ask her if she has any other ideas?'

The bleep was followed by a flood of two-way signing.

Dinah and I hauled ourselves back over the edge of the portal. 'Ready?'

Henry bleeped and Dinah spread her arms wide. We grabbed Henry's top-handle and heaved. After a solid two minutes of hoisting, huffing, panting, grunting, and shifting positions to get a better grip, we managed to pull her over the edge of the doorway. She landed on her side on my leg. While I screamed in agony, Dinah rolled Henry off me. It took us another minute to get her back upright.

I vowed I'd never take accessible buildings for granted again.

I wanted to collapse onto the floor, but Dinah grabbed my hand and led me down the hall to another office. When the door dilated open, I spied Bexley curled up in the corner, snoring.

I climbed over the edge of the portal and knelt down next to her. When I touched her gently on the shoulder, she started. She leapt up and ran in circles around the room. When she finally stopped, she spoke in what sounded like a rapid series of raspberries, clicks, and vibrations.

When I shook my head, she tried again. From the corridor, there was a lengthy stream of angry-sounding bleeps.

I coaxed Bexley into the hallway, helping her over the portal, and then Henry cut her ties. Once we were all free, we searched the building. Not that we got anything to show for our efforts. The whole place was bereft of life. No communication devices. No anything. The occupants had packed up and moved out. Finally.

'I guess there's no need for pussyfooting around the place.' I chuckled at my own joke. 'Should we go to the evac site?'

Bleep. Henry interpreted my question for Dinah. Well, I assumed she did – though for all I know, she was giving her a lecture on macroeconomic theory. Dinah turned to me and raised her little arms wide. Bexley made a very human-like shrug.

When we got to the door to the outside world, three of us climbed over. It was much easier hauling Henry out with Bexley's help.

The world was eerily silent – and darker than I'd imagined. 'Stars!' This wasn't the dark of an oncoming storm, it was the dark of actual night. Or, indeed, of an oncoming asteroid.

Bleep bleep bleep.

I stabbed a finger at Henry. 'Hey, we never agreed what three bleeps meant.'

She still had her two mismatched arms out for talking to Dinah. With one of them, she poked me in the bum – and kept poking me.

'Do you mind?'

Bleep. Poke, poke.

'Yes? Yes, what? Yes, you mind?'

Bleep. Poke, poke, poke.

I moved away from her. Dinah raised an arm and pointed in the direction of the evac site.

Taking the hint, I started walking. Henry stopped poking me.

Bexley talked as much as ever while we walked. At least,

I figured she was talking. She certainly made a lot of noise. Dinah and Henry signed periodically.

As we approached the site, my stomach simultaneously sank and leapt into my throat. Like a miracle of deeply stupid science. The getoffs were gone. Everyone was gone.

'Our pods! Where the galloping gonads are our pods?' Spinning around like a puppy chasing her tail, I tried to spot them.

When I stopped, Bexley was doing the same. Dinah and Henry were just standing there watching us like we were idiots. In fact, when they started signing to one another, I figured that was exactly what they were saying.

Bexley sidled up to me and crossed her arms over her chest. I mirrored her body language. Henry and Dinah had a rapid conversation that excluded us.

'Are you two trying to come up with a plan or are you just mocking us?'

Bleep.

Ugh, right. I'd spent my entire career having open-ended questions drilled into me. Never ask anything that requires just a yes or no, said ... well ... everyone. Only now that was all I had.

'Are you trying to come up with a plan?'

Bleep.

'Are you also mocking us?'

Bleep.

'Fair.' I made a carry-on gesture. Or at least, a gesture that would have meant carry on to a human. Well, to an English-speaking human. And maybe not even that.

'How much time do we have before the asteroid strikes?'

Henry replied with a whole series of vexed-sounding bleeps.

'What? We can do numbers, can't we? Just make a distinct number of bleeps.'

Henry emitted six bleeps.

Oh. 'Six whats? Minutes? Hours?'

Silence.

And then it hit me. 'We don't use the same units of time, do we?'

Bleep bleep.

I blew out a noisy breath. 'How are we going to get home?'

Henry let out a screeching horrible stream of noise.

'Right. I'll just stand here like a useless lump, shall I?'

Bleep.

Bexley whirled around, facing to my left. She spoke rapidly in her language. I couldn't understand anything she said but my eyes followed where she was pointing. A group of plenties was walking up the street towards us. There were more than a dozen of them – and it looked like they were arguing. Still, at least we weren't entirely alone on the planet.

A short white plenti with pale green dots carrying a kitten in her arms tried to run away. A striking person – tall with piebald turquoise and lavender fur – hissed at her. She snatched the kitten from her ... *friend*? Ex? Sibling? Clutching the infant to herself, she ran to us, hissing and bleating. She thrust the child into Bexley's arms.

Bexley said something to her – then turned to the rest of us and said more.

If ever there was a time when we needed our universal translators, this was surely it.

Dinah tentatively approached the group. All the plenties began speaking to her at once – touching her, grabbing at her, vying for her attention.

I sidled up to Henry. 'What's happening?'

Bleep bleep bleep bleeeeeeeeeeeeeeeeeeeeeep!

'Okay, okay. Don't unswear at me like that – I'm still getting the hang of this. Er, it's clear they want something from us, right?'

Bleep.

'They want us to help the kid?'

Bleep.

I pinched the bridge of my nose. This was hard. 'I assume they want us to get them off the planet.'

Bleep. After a pause, Henry added two more bleeps.

I scrunched my eyes closed. 'So … yes but also no?'

Bleep.

All the plenties were speaking rapidly to Dinah. Henry rolled over to them as Bexley backed away and leant against me, still holding the plenti kitten. I put my arm around them both and smiled – trying my best to look reassuring.

Our tender moment didn't last long, though. The plenties pushed past Henry to approach Bexley and me – all mewling, meowing, and hissing at once.

The short plenti with the spots tried to grab the kitten – but the taller one with the turquoise and purple fur got in her way. They shrieked at one another and waved their arms as if they were trying to implore Bexley and me to take one side or the other. All the plenties behind them joined in as well.

My hands shook and my chest tightened. What were we supposed to do? Henry still had a translator; why didn't they speak to her? We were all going to die here in a few hours and they were still trying to argue with us. I wrapped my arms around myself and tried to think – which is hard when you've got people screaming at you and another bleeping an incessant stream of bitterness.

Dinah tapped Henry on the … well, on the lid. She signed something at her. When she finished, Henry turned and tried to address the plenties. But they ignored her, continuing to plead with Bexley and me. At least, I assumed they were pleading.

I was desperate to understand what was happening. Just then Bexley grabbed my sleeve. Babbling excitedly, she pointed up into the sky.

'What am I looking at, Bexley? I don't see anything.'

She tugged her ear and then pointed up again. I tried to follow where she was pointing, but I still couldn't see anything. But then I heard it. The sound of a ship in the atmosphere.

A few moments later, Gracie's orange getoff set down a short walk away from us. The ramp-door swung down as we ran towards it.

BB stepped out, flapping and squawking anxiously.

'Oh, thank God.' I wanted to fall to my knees and cry.

We all ran to them – even the plenties. BB clutched us all tightly, clucking and speaking rapidly. When she finally released us, it was only to beckon us into the ship.

'What's happening? Did Bob kidnap us? I mean, *why* did Bob kidnap us? Can you tell us what these plenties want?'

BB put one of her taloned hands on my shoulder and mimed sitting down and strapping in. She did the same to Bexley then spoke to the assembled plenties. While she did so, Bexley and I boarded the ship. Without translators we were no use outside. I waved at Gracie – or one of her colleagues – swimming in the cockpit pool before helping Bexley strap the kitten into a seat.

Once I was settled, I looked at the scene beyond the vehicle's door. Some of the plenties appeared to be brawling but others were hugging. The tall one with the beautiful fur clung to her short, spotted friend. They got into the getoff together. The spotted one knelt down in front of the kitten and stroked her fur. She kissed the child on the head, touched her partner once more and then left the getoff. The taller one sat down next to her child and strapped herself in.

Two more plenties joined us as Henry and Dinah took their seats. One more climbed in as BB was closing the door. As soon as everyone was safely strapped in, we lifted off.

I don't know how much of it was due to the speed of our launch and the g-force effect and how much of it was the asteroid burning in the atmosphere, but my entire field of vision whited out for a few moments.

When I was able to speak again, I asked, 'Is everything okay? Has everyone been evacuated? How long were we missing? Is the asteroid going to hit soon? And who has our AIs? Did you get them back?'

Henry emitted an ear-piercing torrent of bleeps that shut me up. Bexley clamped her jaw shut at the same time. BB turned towards Henry in her seat and swatted at the offensive robot.

Eventually, I felt the dull thunk of an expert pilot docking with a ship. We all removed our harnesses and stood up. BB went to the cockpit and spoke with Gracie through the glass.

The docking door whooshed open and a blurry black and russet shape flew inwards and jumped into my arms. Spock wiggled and danced and covered me with kisses, her tail a blur.

Spock was closely followed by Elim, who rushed past me and gathered Dinah up in her arms. After a moment, she set the teen down. The two of them moved their hands in rapid signing.

BB indicated to the five plenties that they should remain in their seats. At least, that's what she seemed to be saying.

Before we left the getoff, Dinah approached the cockpit and laid a hand on the glass.

I shrugged and headed for the exit.

As I passed her, the tall turquoise plenti touched my arm. She looked up at me and I could see she wanted to say something. She touched herself and her child then pointed at me as she spoke rapidly. I nodded my head and left the ship.

———

The *Teapot* I returned to was not the one I'd left just a few hours before. For starters, I still couldn't talk to anyone. But also, every room and every corridor was filled with kobolds.

BB said something. I looked at Bexley, who shrugged. BB shook out her feathers and tried again. She held her hands in front of herself in the shape of a bowl and bent over it, miming biting into something.

'Are you asking if we're hungry?' I guessed.

Bexley spoke rapidly – not that I could understand anything she said.

BB's pupils expanded and contracted several times in succession. That was something she did when she was happy.

'Yeah, I'm famished, actually.'

BB turned towards the lift. We followed. Half a dozen kobolds were sitting in the hall, camped out on sleeping bags.

Bleep.

'Are you coming with us, Henry?'

Bleep bleep.

'Okay, we'll see you in a bit, I guess.'

Bleep.

I trailed after BB but then stopped. Turning back, I called out, 'Henry? I'm sorry about having to manhandle you. And I'm sorry I dropped you. I hope I didn't hurt you.'

Bleep bleep.

BB looked at me funny but didn't say anything. Instead of

taking us straight to the kitchen, she walked past it, squeezing between the kobolds sitting on the corridor floor. She led us to the supply room. Even in that tiny space, a few kobolds sat on what looked like camp stools. They took the opportunity to stroke Spock – who was loving all the fuss and attention.

BB rummaged through a few cupboards before she found what she was looking for. When she turned around, she held aloft two collars – identical to the one Spock wore. Turquoise with pale yellow dots.

I looked at BB. 'You want us to take new translators?'

BB held the collars aloft. Both Bexley and I reached out hesitantly.

'I take it you never found ours? The ones we were wearing when … whatever happened.'

Bexley was talking – as ever and always. She was probably saying the same thing I had. Plus a funny story about one of her many dads.

With a sigh, I took a collar and affixed it to myself. Bexley did the same. As soon as I clicked mine into place, it made a series of bleeps.

BB beckoned us to follow her. I excused myself as I stepped over the kobolds as carefully as I could.

When we got to the kitchen, BB fixed us some dinner. Without working translators we couldn't even manage that for ourselves.

Halfway through my spagbol-flavoured nutrient porridge, a mechanical voice announced, 'Reboot complete. Would you like me to apply last known settings?'

'Yeah, Holly. Go ahead.' It was only as I said those words that I realised: Holly was dead.

Long live Holly.

Rincy blinked into existence in the middle of Ten Backwards – the same space where she'd inadvertently subjected us all to tentacle porn a week earlier. The room she was in appeared to be about the size of a transporter pod and it was even more cluttered than what we'd seen of her other spaces.

'Hi, Rincy,' said Bexley. She was sitting on her sleeping bag. All six of us – the *Teapot* crew – were holed up in the only place on the ship the kobolds didn't have free rein. Even Spock had come back up to join us – worn out from the thrill of being the centre of attention.

Henry and Aurora were around on the bridge side of the deck. BB was taking a shower – which meant we were unlikely to see her for another hour or so.

I clutched my mug of helbru to my chest and stroked Spock with my free hand. 'Hey, Rincy. How's it going with the plenties?'

Rincy raised herself up. Her torso was covered in jagged claw marks. Holding her middle arm out of the way, she peeled her chest fur back to reveal glowing orange circuitry. 'Don't even talk to me about the plenties. I cannot wait to be rid of them.' She shuffled around and we heard a clanging as she, presumably, knocked something out of view over.

My hand shot up to my mouth. 'What the hell happened?'

'Oh my gosh,' said Bexley. 'Are you okay? Do you have a doctor – or, like, an engineer – who can fix you up?'

With her middle hand, Rincy closed the wound back up. 'Until we get to Phoebe station, I'm not leaving this room again unless I have to.' She shook her head. 'Anyway, I've alerted the minister. Briefed her on what happened between the two species and with you. She's arranged for a detachment of investigators to rendezvous with us and another set to meet with you at Deep Space Five.'

Bexley shook her head. 'I still can't believe it. Like, I make it a point not to hate people. I don't like hate and I don't like the way it feels to hold it inside me. But I hate those plenties.'

I scooted over closer to her and wrapped an arm around her.

In front of us Rincy wrung three of her hands. 'I know what you mean. It's similar for me. I was designed for pleasure. Not for … this. But I try to remember the whole species isn't bad. At least, they don't have to be. Once the space police have investigated, there will be a trial. The most likely outcome is that the plenties will have to undergo re-education. The kobolds will be offered support for their redevelopment. As a people, they'll probably have to deal with generations of PTSD. But counselling will be made available to them. And I suspect the plenties will be paying restitution for a long time.'

'Wow.' It all seemed so considered and mature – such a

grownup way to deal with crime. Which reminded me...
'What about Bob?'

'After you lot disappeared,' Rincy said, 'Bob called me in
floods of tears. She told me there had been a freak accident –
that a bus on its way to the evacuation site had accidentally
run you down. She said you'd all been killed.' We'd heard
this second-hand from Aurora and BB, of course. 'I wanted
to collect your bodies. But she said there was no time. She
urged us to load up the ships and leave. She even tried to
seize control of the *Egg*.'

Bexley and I both gasped. We hadn't heard this part. We
knew that they'd kidnapped us and tied us all up and
removed our translators – well, all except Henry. They'd just
dumped her. They didn't think to tie her up or remove her
translator because they didn't believe she was a person.

'What? How did you...' began Bexley. 'I mean, what...
How did you... What happened?'

'Oh, they stormed the bridge and demanded we stop the
asteroid instead of evacuating them. Ridiculous, really. But
the crew of the *Egg* are experienced in dealing with space
pirates. They had them all safely restrained within an hour.'
She shook herself out. 'Anyways, we've got a few people in
the brig on the *Egg* – Bob and the old plenti who kept that
infant kobold captive. A few others who've been accused of
specific crimes against individual kobolds. Oh, and Apple
was the one who hacked your AI, Lem. She's in the brig as
well.'

'Huh,' was all I could think to say.

'How is Helo, by the way?' asked Rincy.

Bexley smiled. 'I spoke to BB a few minutes ago. Helo's
improving. BB and the kobold doctor are treating her. She's
malnourished and she has some broken ribs. But she's getting

the treatment she needs. She never learnt to sign, so she's starting now. And BB discovered that she loves to sing, so she's been teaching her some peri tunes. Helo can't form the words but she has a beautiful voice.'

'Sounds like she's doing as well as can be expected.' Rincy leaned back against the wall. 'It was a successful mission – even if it didn't turn out quite as expected. We got everyone out safely – well, everyone who chose to leave. And that's what matters.'

'Yeah, I suppose.' Part of me was still grieving for Holly – even though the new Holly didn't seem to notice it wasn't the same AI it had been previously.

'How are things on the *Teapot*?'

I nodded. 'It's as crowded as you might expect. But it's good. Everything's going smoothly.'

Bexley snorted noisily. 'Lem's just happy she's got people who want to play Kobold in the Basement with her.'

I grinned. There was some truth to that. Some of the kobolds had taken to Dungeons and Dragons like naturals. They'd taught me a similar game from their world too.

Bexley shifted and sat upright. 'Thanks for getting in touch, Rincy. It's been good talking to you. I'm sure we'll work with you again sometime.'

Rincy bobbed her head. 'Of course. And no doubt I'll see you at the inquest – whenever that is.'

'We will. Take care of yourself until then. Bye.'

———

Ten days later, the *Teapot* gang all walked, rolled, or floated into the pub. It was one of the kobold-owned establishments that had popped up all over the station in the week since we'd arrived. A cloud of small kobolds trailed after Spock.

Guinan was working the bar. She waved at us in greeting. 'Good evening. Welcome to the White Hart. Please take a seat and place your orders via your personal devices.'

I pulled my shiny, new phone from my pocket and admired it. It wasn't the same as the one I'd lost. But I'd been able to sync it to the last backup of my original mobile. So, this non-Earth device now had an extensive selection of Earth science fiction and fantasy novels. And my music collection.

'Excellent,' said Guinan. 'Like I said, please take a seat anywhere you find species-appropriate arrangements.'

We selected a table and picked our respective spots to sit, stand, perch, or hover. Those of us who ate studied the menu on our devices.

'That's one thing I miss when we're on the *Teapot*,' I said.

'Real food,' chorused everyone.

I scowled. 'It's not that I don't like the nutrient porridge. It's just that—'

'You miss real fruit and veg.' Again with the chorus.

Henry had taken to keeping her two jury-rigged arms at the ready whenever we were out and about on Deep Space Five. It made it easier to communicate directly with the kobolds. 'Are you even aware of how often you repeat yourself, sandwich?'

'Ooh, speaking of sandwiches... I know what I'm ordering.' Real bread was something else we didn't get enough of in space.

'Hey, look who it is,' squealed Bexley. 'Elim, Dinah, over here!'

From across the crowded pub, two kobolds raised their hands in greeting.

Chairs shaped for kobolds had appeared all over the station. The population had more than doubled overnight when we arrived. Kobolds were now working in almost every industry on the station. And they were the majority of the customers too.

Dinah and Elim grabbed chairs for themselves and hauled them over to our table. We all budged up to make space.

'You're sure you don't mind if we join you?' asked Elim. 'I thought you might want some time away from us.'

'You are very welcome,' said Aurora.

'Believe me.' Bexley touched a hand to her still short – but now stylishly so – mane. 'You folks were the best guests we've had on the ship. I mean, sure, there were a gazillion of you, which made privacy a bit hard to come by for a few days. But that's a small price to pay compared to what your people have endured.'

We all turned to Dinah – who grinned impishly. 'You're waiting for me to interpret for her, aren't you?' She tapped the corner of her new glasses.

Over the last day or so, a lot of kobolds had started wearing specs. I'd assumed it was some sort of fashion craze. Or maybe they didn't have the best vision. But now that I looked closely, I spied a faint yellow glow on the lenses.

Bexley practically leapt out of her seat. 'Oh my gosh! Are those the HUDs we were talking about during the trip? They're amazing. I've seen loads of people wearing them around the station.' She stood behind Dinah and Elim, trying to see through their lenses. 'They're smart glasses! You sync them up to your personal AI and then they can overlay translations onto the screen. They translate auditory language into visual signals.'

'Oh, wow. That's so cool.' I knew a few people back on Earth who would love to get their hands on a pair of those.

There was a brief lull in the conversation as Guinan dropped off our drinks. I took a sip of my pint. It wasn't quite beer – but it was pretty close. Someone told me it was made from fermented mushrooms. Near enough.

BB clucked her beak. 'So, Dinah… Have you heard anything?'

Dinah looked like she was busting at the seams to share her news. She spread her arms wide. 'I got in!'

BB jumped up and hugged her. Aurora glowed green. Elim put her arm protectively on her child's shoulders.

'Are you going to fill us in, kid?' asked Henry – more gently than I'd heard her speak to anyone.

'BB helped me apply to medical school on Quoth. I got the news this afternoon – I start in about three months.'

We all congratulated her.

'I'll continue apprenticing with our doctor until it's time to go. I could stay and do that instead of going to Quoth, but I want to learn multi-species medicine.'

'The whole family is going with her,' said Elim, still clutching Dinah.

Dinah beamed. 'Elim's spouses and her other house-offspring and their partners are coming. We're all going to be able to reconnect and get to know one another all over again.'

'Even my egg-offspring – Dinah's egg-parent,' Elim signed. 'We're all going to Quoth while Dinah does her studies.'

'That's brilliant,' I said.

Bexley got up and hugged Dinah. 'Well done, you.'

Dinah looked up at Bexley. 'What about you? What are your plans?'

Bexley glanced at the rest of us before answering. 'Well, I did get a message from two of my dads this afternoon inviting us all to come and stay with them for a bit.' She turned to look at me and the other Teapotters. 'And we did promise we'd take a bit of a break after this mission. What do you say?'

THE END (FOR NOW)

Lem and the whole *Teapot* crew will be back later in 2022. Sign up to my newsletter to get updates. And you'll get free stories as well.

If you'd like to read about Lem's life on Earth – including how she first met Spock – click below.

PSST! WANT A FREE BOOK?

Click the image above to get Stardust Wake for free

ACKNOWLEDGEMENTS

Towards the end of 2020, I decided I just … couldn't. I couldn't face another serious novel about serious people dealing with serious problems.

And so instead, I sat down to write something excessively silly. That something silly turned into *The Left Hand of Dog*, the first book in the *Starship Teapot* series.

And then I had an idea for the second book. But when I sat down to write it, what came out was much darker than I'd intended. How does a person try to write a bit of lightweight, easy-reading space opera only to have it turn into an essay about slavery, genocide, and oppression?

I don't know – but that's exactly what happened.

I worked hard to get the balance right: the darkness of the themes and the lightness of the tone. My aim is always to address real issues but to do so in a way that has warmth and heart – that respects the sanctity of life and the rights of people. I want to write stories that are diverse and inclusive at their very core.

Did I achieve those aims? I hope so, but I'm sure some of you will say no. If your reasons for disliking this story include the terms 'political correctness' or 'SJW', then … shrug. You're not my audience. On the other hand, if you didn't like this story because you think it should have been more inclusive or because I should have tried harder to avoid the white saviour trope, I'd love to hear from you. I'm always striving to learn more, to do better, to *be* better than I was yesterday. Please get in touch.

Isabelle Felix got stuck right into the guts of my ridiculous tale – revealing the flaws, pointing out where I'd done exactly what I said I was trying to avoid, drawing out the details I'd invariably glossed over, and asking me all the right questions. If you ever find yourself in need of a perceptive and conscientious beta/sensitivity reader, I highly recommend her.

I couldn't have written that 'Lizard in the Basement' chapter without Titaania's help. She was fabulous to work with and helped me create that ridiculous game.

The WiFi Sci-Fi writers' group has been the most amazing gift. They continually teach, push, and cheerlead me to be a better writer.

I also want to thank J. Scott Coatsworth for being one of the biggest cheerleaders of diverse and inclusive science fiction on Earth.

The gorgeous cover art for this book was created by Vadim Sadovski. Isn't it fab? He's so talented and I was lucky to work with him.

I'm phenomenally grateful to have such a great editing team. My first stop in editing this book was Michelle Meade. Michelle has worked with a host of best-selling and award-winning authors ... and me. I'm so grateful that she makes time in her schedule for an unknown like me.

Lucy Rose York dug into the meat of this vegetarian story to make it the best version of itself it could be. She provided expert copy-editing services. And, as always, Hannah McCall of Black Cat Editorial Services provided expert proofreading. Any mistakes you find now are because I forgot to incorporate her corrections.

Finally, my legally contracted lifemate, Dave, has been

putting up with more than any human being should have to. If you've ever met me in real life, you'll understand what a big deal that is. Seriously ... I'm *a lot*. Dave has listened to me talk about my imaginary friends every single day for four years. Dave's the best person.

Photo © Lex Fleming

SI CLARKE is a misanthrope who lives in Deptford, *sarf ees* London. She shares her home with her partner and an assortment of waifs and strays. When not writing convoluted, inefficient stories, she spends her time telling financial services firms to behave more efficiently. When not doing either of those things, she can be found in the pub or shouting at people online – occasionally practising efficiency by doing both at once.

As someone who's neurodivergent, an immigrant, and the proud owner of an invisible disability, she strives to present a realistically diverse array of characters in her stories.

 twitter.com/clacksee

instagram.com/clacksee_author

goodreads.com/clacksee

bookbub.com/authors/si-clarke

ALSO BY SI CLARKE

Find a complete list of my books on my website at whitehartfiction.co.uk/books.

If you get books directly from me, you'll get 20% off with the code 'JUDGEMENT'.

REVIEWS

If you enjoyed this story, please consider leaving a review on Goodreads or Readerly or the ebook retailer of your choosing.

KEEP IN TOUCH

Join my newsletter for:

- snippets from what I'm working on;
- photos of my dogs;
- reviews of books I've enjoyed recently;
- links to promos focusing on diverse and inclusive speculative fiction; and
- more free stories from me.

whitehartfiction.co.uk/newsletter